MW01712861

A Small Place in the Sun

Kay

A Small Place in the Sun

Patrick O'Flaherty

Breakwater Books
277 Duckworth Street
P. O. Box 2188
St. John's, Newfoundland
A1C 6E6

Cover illustration by Angela King-Harris

The Publisher gratefully acknowledges the support of The Canada Council.

The Publisher acknowledges the financial contribution of the Cultural Affairs Division of the Department of Culture, Recreation and Youth, Government of Newfoundland and Labrador, which has helped make this publication possible.

Canadian Cataloguing in Publication Data

O'Flaherty, Patrick, 1939 -
A small place in the sun
Short stories.
ISBN 0-920911-70-6

I. Title.
PS8579.F52S62 1989 C813'.54 C89-098560-X
PR9199.3.034S62 1989

Table of Contents

A small place in the sun

That there were deep differences between his family and some of their neighbours became clear to Jimmy Byrne about ten o'clock one night in the late summer of his eighth year, when Ken Slade came by for a visit. Mr. Slade lived only a quarter of a mile away, but he was a man who kept to himself, and his wife Fanny was delicate. It was strange for anyone to come in the house at such a late hour, let alone him.

"I allowed this mornin' there was goin' t' be trouble," Granny Byrne said when she heard the latch lift on the porch door. The old black horse named Dandy had come right up to the kitchen window just after daylight and looked in. That meant the worst kind of luck. It might even be a death in the house. "Now look what we got," she said. "A stranger."

"Oh, Christ, Ma, it's only Ken," Jimmy's father said when he saw who it was. He got up from the settle where he'd been napping and spent a few minutes talking to the visitor about the fishery. "Hauled twelve fleets of lines this morning and got twenty-five codfish," he said. "My dear man, this place is finished. I got around forty, forty-five quintals out in the store, that's all. Never seen the like of it. No herring worth a damn, either. And the few salmon I got in the spring I had to sell to Art Champion for fifteen cents a pound. She's gone bottom up, head over heels."

"That's Long Beach for you," his wife Molly said as she lifted a damper on the kitchen stove and poked the fire. It was already starting to get cold in the evenings. She gave him a look. "Told you, didn't I?" He made no answer, but only rubbed his eyes.

Then he said to one and all: "Down on your knees." This too was strange, for the rosary, taken up vigorously in May month, had been given up for the summer. But now the sorrowful mysteries were dutifully intoned, though not without murmurs from the five children, who were getting used to playing Chinese checkers and listening to the radio before their mother sent them off to bed. By the Carrying of the Cross, Colin, who was nine and should have known better, had been slapped by Granny Byrne for kneeling on the cat's tail; and even Alphonsus, going on twelve, had to have his ear pulled for pinching his sister Elizabeth and making her squeal. The Hail Holy Queen came none too soon, and Jimmy, not having stirred from his place on the kitchen floor because experience had taught him it was best to leave your knees in one spot, turned to look at the clock on the mantelpiece. Would he miss the start of the Cisco Kid? was what he was thinking. He was surprised by what he saw. In the straight-backed chair by the washstand sat Mr. Slade, head bowed, hands buried deep in the pockets of his overalls. Not only was he sitting up, but he wasn't even saying "poor banished children of Eve" or sending up sighs with the rest of them. No holy rosary for him.

His mother later explained to Jimmy what Mr. Slade was, and when he looked around the church next Sunday, sure enough, he could see that the Slade children, Harold and Gwendolyn, weren't present. Nor were Winston Reynolds and George Dale, two more chums. Well, not chums exactly, in the way that Will Joe Hogan was a chum. Jimmy didn't throw rocks at the birds or at the bottles on the telegraph poles with them, or go in the woods in their company to catch trout or pick berries. If he had gone to school with them—and he now knew why he didn't—it might have been different. But when he went to the sandy beach in Northern Bay, a mile up the shore, on Sunday afternoons to swim in the fresh-water pool or lie around under the hot sun, he would see them and talk to them. Sometimes, they would all walk back together from the sands. They were all right, especially Gwendolyn, who said she was getting a sun tan. "I'd sun tan her if I owned her," Molly said. He liked going up to Northern Bay, because that was where his mother came from and he had uncles and cousins there.

In the fall his father gave up fishing early and went to Halifax to work on the docks. His letters home were filled with adventures. Once a woman with blonde hair came up to him on Barrington Street and caught hold of him. He had a job to get clear of her, he wrote. When he had trouble sleeping, he got pills from a German doctor. A German doctor in Halifax, and the war only just over! He stayed in his boarding house most nights because he heard what had happened in Halifax on V-E Day; the streets weren't safe. Through what his family gathered was some kind of masterful stroke, he had managed to get in the union when others couldn't and, being thought of as Irish, was well liked. He could go down to Boston if he wanted to and work on the docks. He was half tempted to move his whole family to the States. There was more money to be made there than in

Canada. "I'm liable to send down for you any old day," he wrote. "All you have to have is an Irish name, and you got it made with the union. You're in like Flynn. They look after you." Molly, who had once been a teacher, explained what a union was. The house was full of grand talk.

Early in the spring their cow got sick with milk fever, and Alphonsus found her lying shivering on the cold stable floor. All efforts to get her on her feet were in vain. The new calf had to be fed with a bottle and kept in the porch of the house until the cow got better. *If* she got better. Ebe Tucker from Burnt Point, three miles down the shore, was sent for. He said the only way to save her was to pump her up. It was a new way to treat milk fever. It had worked on two of his cows, and he couldn't see why it wouldn't work on one from Long Beach. "Cows are all the same, not like people," he said. He wanted an answer straightaway; was he to do it or wasn't he? He was a busy man. Granny Byrne shook her head. "Pump!" she snorted. "What next, what next!"

But Molly said "Go ahead," and while skeptical neighbours who had, with Granny, advised other treatments looked on, Mr. Tucker got a pump from his truck and pumped air into the cow's udder through each of her tits. Jimmy watched from a distance with Gwendolyn. "Tit is not a nice word," she said. A day later the cow was up on her legs eating hay and the calf was back in the stable. Jimmy and Colin made sure that her pen was swept out every day and the calf had a good place to lie down. They gave Dandy's pen a good cleaning, too, because it had been neglected during the cow's sickness. After shovelling the manure out from under him, they cleaned off his legs and sides with the horse comb.

Then something even worse happened. Their sister Lucy got sick with diarrhea and vomiting, and started to lose weight. The doctor came down twice from Western Bay, far up the shore, to look at her, but couldn't do anything to help. Molly, afraid that Lucy was going to die, sent a wire to

Halifax from the post office in Northern Bay, and back their father came in May, bringing bottles of cod liver oil and B-1 tonic, a bag of oranges, miraculous medals, and renewed devotion to the rosary. "Down on your knees," he said an hour after he landed in the house. Later in the night, Jimmy woke up to hear his parents saying the sorrowful mysteries again in their bedroom. Sure enough, Lucy started getting better right away and was soon out of bed and playing in the kitchen. All hands were now wearing medals around their necks, even the cow and calf. They needed looking after too, his father said.

He brought something else with him from Halifax: a money belt filled with banknotes. Not trusting banks, he had kept all his savings under the mattress in his boarding house, and the evening after he came back he counted it on the kitchen table in front of his family: $1,700. As a fisherman, he was used to living on credit. Now he had money. He fingered it, stacked the bills on top of each other. What would he do with it all? Fishing had brought him only hard work and misery. He didn't want to start that again. If he did, he'd lose the little bit of hair he had left on his head after Halifax. "A shop!" said Molly. "Let's start a little shop up on the road. There's no place to buy a pound of sugar in Long Beach. We're halfway between the big dealers. Ron Woodfine and Will Johnson might deal with us. And we'd get a bit of money from the children going back and forth to school. The only thing we have in this hole is the school."

She forgot the church, which was in Long Beach too. Jimmy noticed that she didn't mention Ken Slade. Wouldn't he deal with them? He lived no further away than the Johnsons and Woodfines.

This was something, a Byrne owning a shop! His father fell back on the settle with his hands clasped behind his head, sized up the money, looked out through the window towards the salt water, and burst out laughing. He laughed a lot. Then he turned serious. "I'll have to ask somebody about this," he said. "Not the priest," said Molly. Granny Byrne jumped out of the rocking chair and went to the stove, where somebody had left the cover off the teapot. "More trouble and torment," she said.

The next day was Saturday. His father took Jimmy with him and walked down to see Marmaduke Tucker, the merchant who owned Thomas Tucker and Sons Limited. Jimmy hadn't been down as far as Burnt Point before, but he knew that was the place they had the parade every July, led by the man on the white horse. His father was dressed up in his new blue serge suit of clothes and quiff hat. He had a bit of style about him since his trip to Halifax. Everyone said so.

It was a long walk on the dusty road, and Jimmy was tired when they got to the shop. A big car was in front of the door, and a crowd of men and boys looked at them as they went in. What a shop it was! Jimmy could see shelf upon shelf of tins, boxes, bottles, dishes, pans, dry goods, everything. The really special thing, he knew from his mother, was in dry goods, but he wasn't in a rush and the whole shop was fun to look at. Besides, it was nice to put things off. He watched the clerks at work, serving the customers. When you wanted a piece of line to tie up a parcel, all you had to do was reach up and pull some down from a reel about ten feet above the counter. It was easy to break the line by hooking it around your thumb and hauling. There was one shelf with nothing on it but tinned spaghetti, his favourite meal. A big ham and an even bigger cheese lay on the counter, but someone would be sure to notice if you tried to cut a piece off with a pocketknife. He hadn't brought his pocketknife with him, and anyway, it would be wrong. But Will Joe Hogan would have a piece if he was here. A delicious smell of apples made his mouth water. He could see the apples in a box, the ones on top nice and shiny, and the ones in the next tier wrapped in pieces of paper.

After twenty minutes or so Duke Tucker appeared, spoke to his father, took the quiff and put it on his own head, and led them off towards a room at the back. "You wait in the shop, sonny," the merchant said. "We'll only be in the office a half-hour." The door closed, and Jimmy couldn't see what they were doing, because the little window in the door was too high. He soon got tired of standing and decided to sit down on a box, but a man serving customers shouted from inside the counter, "Hey, get your ass off that, that's sweet biscuits." If his father was out here, he wouldn't be yelled at like that, he thought. But he got up and walked over to the front door, since it wasn't time yet for the special treat. It soon would be. A boy about his own size looked in at him and stuck out his tongue. At first Jimmy didn't recognize him because the glass in the door was dirty, but then he saw it was Harold Slade. Harold stuck out his tongue again and made a fist at him. Then he grabbed his crotch and pulled it up and down as if he were trying to tear it loose, all the while shaking his fist with the free hand. Other boys stood around on the steps, pointing inside and laughing, grabbing their crotches too. "See any horses?" one of them yelled at him. What did that mean? Should he go out and ask? It was a mystery.

Something happened to him then. He felt that he was inside the door and would never get through it. He was shut in, cut off. As he stared out, he could feel the medal hanging around his neck and was glad it was inside his shirt where nobody would notice it. "See any horses?" a laughing boy screamed. Jimmy looked down the road through the big window in front of the shop and saw, not horses, but Gwendolyn playing hopscotch with three girls. She was jumping up and down and clapping her hands. When her dress bounced up, he could see her naked legs above her stockings. He thought she must have cousins down here.

Recovering himself, he at last went over to dry goods and looked at the toys in the glass case. He had already decided what he wanted to be when he grew up. No fishing boat for him, his father said; if Alphonsus took up doctoring, he might go into teaching. That was a good racket, too. His mother ruled out Christian brothers or priests. But he had his own secret hopes. Now he feasted his eyes on the glittering six-shooters, and dreamed of fleeing bandits, sunlit canyons, beautiful senoritas rescued from danger, and white stallions.

He was still there, nose to the glass, an hour later when the two men came out of the office, talking loudly about Canada and the baby bonus. "Long Beach'll have no worries when the baby bonus comes," Mr. Tucker said, "you can mark that down." They were both red in the face, and Jimmy hadn't seen his father grin this way before. "What's your name, sonny?" Mr. Tucker said to him and, on getting the reply "James Byrne, sir," called out to the man who had ordered him off the biscuit box, "Harry, give old Jim here a candy." Harry came over and gave him a peppermint knob, which he put in his breeches' pocket. "So I'll be talking to you later, Paddy," Mr. Tucker said as they went out through the door. But his father had to go back to the office to get the quiff. Then they went out again.

There was nobody outside now because it had started to rain. The wind was up too; they leaned into it and started back up the shore. At a couple of places on the walk, his father had to go into the woods by the side of the road. Jimmy thought he could smell B-1 tonic off him. He knew his mother would be mad with them because they got their shoes so dirty. But Jimmy wasn't mad. Although he was a big boy, before they got to Long Beach he reached out and took his father's hand. For the first time he noticed how rough and hard it was. He held on tight until they got home.

These, thy gifts

Liam Redmond and Bridget Oliver got married young and, while still in their twenties, had three sons. Liam's job in the civil service consisted mostly of pushing paper off his desk onto somebody else's, but he worked hard in hopes of advancement. "If you work hard, someone above you will take notice," he would tell his boys. His boys were his life. He read stories to them at bedtime when they were tiny, made stories up when there were no books around to read, taught them their prayers, took them to church, drove them to parks, summer camps, and fishing spots, and when they began school, prepared their lunches and made sure they ate them. His and Bride's marriage was a modern one. She wanted a career too, and the agreement they made was that if she cooked dinner, he would handle lunch duty. Other tasks were to be shared as well. "There will be no cafeteria lunches for my boys," he said. "They're coming home to have a proper meal." And so he made arrangements to come back from work at noon, and gave them lunches of toasted cheese sandwiches, real spaghetti, omelettes, fat hamburgers, and, on rare occasions, hot dogs. This was in his early years. As he got busier pushing paper, he depended more on tinned food and macaroni.

"The important thing is that their father is here for them," he told Bride. "They can discuss things with me. They can make contact."

"Discuss what things?" she asked one day.

"Ideas, books, problems they might run into. I want to do this right. They have to know about ideas."

"There's more to life than opinions," she replied.

He thought she made this comment to provoke him. "I'm worried about safety, too," he said.

After lunch he would drive them back to school. He gave each of them strict instructions about getting into cars with men who offered rides home in the afternoon. They were to accept rides only from blood relatives. If this meant they had to walk home in rain, snow, or sleet, so be it. If they broke a leg, they had to crawl home. He had this drilled into them and it became a game. They even had a name on it.

"Will you take a ride from a teacher?" he would ask.

"No."

"From a priest?"

"No."

"From a bishop?"

"No."

"Not even an Anglican bishop?"

"Especially not from an Anglican bishop."

"From the father of your best friend?"

"No."

"From whom, pray, will you accept a ride?"

A shout: "Only from a blood relative!"

He would then hug them and let them out of the car to go into the schoolyard. This, too, was in the early years. Bride hated the bishop game from the start, claiming it made the children mistrustful. "Mistrustful!" he would shoot back. "Look, I'm starting to have doubts about the relatives, too. It's a tough world those kids are going into. It's my job to see they're ready for it."

He saw it as his duty to protect them from crackpots and incompetents in the classrooms, and made a point of going to all P.T.A. meetings and interviewing sessions at the schools. He checked out the backgrounds of the teachers and principals, and looked for signs in the boys' homework that the teachers were starting to slack off or get weird. Men were turning strange everywhere, behaving like barnyard animals. Rape and child molesting cases were reported in the paper every day. A father couldn't be too careful.

A teacher of his second son, Liam Jr., held a meeting of Grade One parents and asked for permission to use the strap. Each parent was asked to give formal approval. The four who spoke before Liam said that in certain circumstances the strap, carefully administered, was a needed corrective to juvenile mischievousness. They didn't object to it. "Hit my son once," Liam said when his turn came, "with a strap or anything else, and you'll be in court pretty goddamn fast. That's my opinion, and you'd better listen to it." The teacher had been in training for the priesthood and had carried an air of sanctimoniousness with him from the seminary.

"I'm only thinking of what's best for the child, Mr. Redmond," he said as the discussion broke up. He had a long, sedate, horse-like face, hard to read.

"I'll decide what's best for my sons, if you don't mind," said Liam. The next day he requested, and was granted, a transfer to another class for his boy. Bride said he was becoming a pain to the principal and the school board, but he didn't care. "Let them do their jobs," he said, "and they'll get no trouble from me."

As his boys grew older, Liam became expert in devising ways to keep them occupied during long drives to the country or at Sunday dinner with relatives. Mind games were his specialty. The mind was a muscle, he kept saying, and had to be exercised to grow, just like an arm or leg.

"I'll make sure they can speak out and think and argue," he said. "That'll be my gift to them. Nobody knows how to argue any more."

"Argue about what?" asked Bride.

"Oh, politics, social reform, bigotry, issues."

On the highway he might drive up behind a car with a Massachusetts licence plate and say, "I am not driving behind a car with Massachusetts licence plates." The boys would then have to explain in what way this was an accurate observation. The one to get the answer—and they knew from experience that there always was an answer—would be given a prize. To test their memories, he would stop the car before entering a familiar curve and demand to know what lay beyond it. A pond? Claypit? Sideroad? What? Memory was a part of intelligence, he would say if Bride protested. Developing it would make them smarter.

When these games palled, he would tell stories and ask, "What is the meaning of that?" Aesop, fairy tales, poetry, and the Bible were plundered for good, pithy stories. There had to be a point to them; otherwise they were no good. When they couldn't see the meaning of a story, he would reveal it. He told them why the man who came into the vineyard at the eleventh hour was thought by some to deserve as much as those who had come in early and borne the burden and heat of the day, adding that this was an opinion he personally found difficult to share. He told them how to go about making friends among the Mammon of wickedness, and how necessary it was for them to do this as they were R.C.s in a province dominated by a greedy Protestant elite. He explained why Satan could claim the whole world as his property, a claim that seemed more and more reasonable as time passed. And he told them of his own childhood, and of his father's adventures as a fisherman, sealer, and stevedore. His father was a knockabout Newfoundlander who could turn his hand to anything.

It was these stories about their grandfather that the boys loved best. Their favourite was the one about the softball. One hot day when Liam was ten, he and his brother Frank were forbidden to go up the road to play a softball game they had been eagerly looking forward to, because they had to help put caplin on the potato garden behind their house. The work was so important, and so hard, that the whole family lent a hand. Even the fishery was set aside for the day. Each trench in the garden was plowed up, and then the loose earth was shovelled on the caplin that had earlier been spread along the beds of potato plants. You might also have to pick up a few dry, shrivelled, potato stalks, left over from last fall, as you shovelled.

At midday, their young horse that was toiling alongside them suddenly took fright, tore the reins from Frank's hands and the plow from their father's, went galloping through the garden and meadow with the plow slamming behind still on the traces, crashed through a fence, and ended up half a mile away, bruised and exhausted, foaming at the mouth. In careering through the yard in front of the house, the horse and what was left of the plow just missed Liam's two little sisters. Their father retrieved the frightened animal and finished the work with a plow borrowed from a neighbour. He was fond of the horse, but had to tie him to a fence and give him a licking with a small picket.

The job didn't get finished until the late afternoon. Before going in to supper, the weary fisherman said to Liam,

"Go get your bat and ball." He had never before offered to play softball, though he said that he had played many games in his months in Halifax, and that after his experiences working on the docks there as a young man, the world had little new left to show him. Frank took the bat, and his father let loose with the first and only pitch Liam ever saw him throw—overhand, and straight through the kitchen window, sending shards of glass over the stove and floor and knocking the sugar bowl off the table. Liam's mother made a fuss about the bowl, which had been a wedding gift, but his father got a big charge out of what happened. "It's only a bowl," he said to her. When he saw Frank and Liam going off to play softball later in the summer, he would sometimes say, "There's not much to that game. I might come up and play it one of these days." But he never did. Nor did he ever interfere with their softball plans from that day. He said he was a believer in sports as a builder of character.

"What does that story mean, Dad?" Liam's oldest boy, Tim, asked one day.

"Oh, it's only a story," he said. But sometimes he wondered.

Liam also believed in sports, and was excited when Tim started to play hockey. The equipment was expensive, and there was the nuisance of having the skates sharpened every week; but Liam didn't complain. After driving Tim to the early morning practices, he would lace his skates up and make sure the helmet was snug before sending him on the ice. Tim was no great skater, and in Atom hockey sometimes sat on the bench in big games and in the playoffs. Liam chafed at this and over dinner would say, "Work hard when you're on the ice, and complain when you're left on the bench. Don't give in, fight on. They'll find a use for a boy like you if you stand up for yourself. They'll notice you after a while." After years of being in the same job, Liam was beginning to think he hadn't complained enough. Some of the younger crowd were getting ahead of him.

"Fight on?" said Bride. "Is this a war he's in? He's a kid, for God's sake. A kid playing a game."

"He's a Redmond," said Liam. "That's an Irish name. There's no inside track for him. Listen to me, I know this."

Tim's talents turned out to be courage and tenacity, and by his Peewee years he had become known for his willingness to get in front of the opponents' net to deflect hard shots from the point, and to mix it up in the corners. When a fight broke out, he was usually not far off. "If someone nails you, don't skate away," Liam told him. In one tough 3-2 victory, two shots bounced in off his legs and he was credited with both goals. He was a hero that day. Liam went to as many games as he could and shouted advice from the sidelines, making sure the coaches could see he was taking note of the players who were on the bench. He also joined the parents' hockey committee. If you weren't on the committee, your son didn't stand a chance in the league. He was overjoyed to see a gradual improvement in Tim's stickhandling and skating. Watching hockey became a big part of his life. Enthusiasm over athletics led him to consider the shape he and Bride were in. Soon, he was out jogging in new running shoes and shorts.

Time slipped by so fast that before he knew it, his son was out of the Peewees. In Tim's first Bantam season some men still went into the dressing room to get their boys, but most stood around outside fingering their car keys and talking hockey politics. The last time Liam went in was after a big win just before Christmas. It had been a day of drudgery at his office. Tim was sitting at the end of a long bench in the sweaty, noisy room, and Liam had to walk over sticks, stockings, and jock straps to get to him and give him a pat of encouragement. No coach or other adult was in evidence. He noticed that as he moved through the room, the conversation got a little quieter. A couple of players turned their backs to put on their shorts. Two or three kept up their horseplay. One stamped out a cigarette.

"How are you, Mr. Redmond?" a boy noted for his politeness asked.

"Fine, just fine, Stephen," said Liam. "Good game, pal," he said to Tim. "Real good. Nice check you dished out to their big guy, though I didn't like the way he decked you later. What's his name? Brown? Barlow?" He had half a mind to speak to the fellow after the game and tell him to keep his stick down.

"His name's Bartlett," a boy said. "He's their captain. He's getting a tryout with Verdun next year."

"The best player in St. John's," Stephen added. "No question."

Tim spoke up: "Dad, will you go out and get me a coke and a bag of chips?"

"Sure, son. Everything ok?" Tim nodded.

Liam went outside and bought the coke and chips at the canteen. Returning, he held the dressing room door slightly ajar and noted that the noise and roughhouse had picked up. Then he decided to stay outside in the corridor.

It was late in the afternoon, and with Christmas approaching the stadium was little used. The other fathers had drifted off to watch the ice being cleaned, and as he leaned against the wall and waited he could see the whole length of the concrete corridor, which was cold, dreary, and, for the moment, empty of life. Yet behind two of the doors leading off it could be heard the joyous shouts of children at play. He suddenly felt desolate. He thought of his father. Had there been such a corridor stretching off for him thirty years ago? And did he know he would have to walk through it?

After the season was over, the team fathers gave a party for the players and coaches, presented leather jackets to the boys, awarded trophies, and had Kentucky Fried chicken brought in. It all cost a pretty penny. The chairman of the hockey executive in the school, a guidance counselor named Joseph Breen, gave a speech about the value of being a good sport even if you didn't always win. Coming second, as the boys had done this year, was no disgrace in his eyes or in the school's eyes, he said. The game itself was not the important thing. The important thing was getting along with your fellow students and feeling good about yourself. "What I hear these lads saying," he said, "is that they want to feel good about themselves, about their school, and about all the players in the league." After this, he reported at length on the financial situation facing the committee at year's end, from which it appeared that much fund-raising would have to be undertaken over the summer months. This could only be done by the parents through selling tickets on donated merchandise and, if they wanted, by holding bingo games. Maybe they should also open a booth at the regatta in August. He would leave all this in their capable hands.

He then gave many reasons for what he regarded as a serious step, but a step he was nevertheless willing to recommend: taking the team out of the league altogether and forming a new division with only three teams, all from within the school. This would lessen the emphasis on competition, he said. As this sank in, the fathers, well fortified now from pocket flasks, at first seemed equally divided on the proper course of action to take on the recommendation, but in time those favouring withdrawal from the league gained the upper hand. Discussion grew animated. Many rose to deliver their views. Being a non-drinker, Liam felt out of place and said nothing. As he sat back, he realized how much time he spent these days listening: to half-educated chairmen of committees; teachers who couldn't teach; preachers who couldn't preach; placemen, compromisers, bootlickers, backstairs men. The dunces had gained the ascendancy; he found himself off the main track, shunted. How had it happened? Was his the right way? How could he shield his boys from all this?

Looking around the cafeteria, he saw that the hockey players were on one side of the room and the fathers on the other. The boys were giggling and kicking one another under the tables as each speaker rose and droned on, and when Mr. Breen returned to the podium and brought the discussion to an end with a plea for all present to keep sharing feelings about their experiences as they had done this evening, there was much shouting and thumping.

"Good speech, Mr. Breen," Stephen, the polite boy, said.

"You should be in the UN, Joe," Liam heard his son yell. Later, he saw Tim talking to the counselor in a corner. They had a chuckle over something. "He's a laugh—Mr. Breen," Tim said afterwards in the car.

That night Liam talked to Bride about a new idea he had. Why didn't the two of them get skates next fall and try to stay in shape that way? "Who says I'm out of shape?" she said, glaring at him. No, it was too late for her to go back to skating. He could take it up if he wanted to, but leave her out of it. Her job and her family were enough for her to handle. Today at work the boss had handed her a message to call the principal about Liam Jr., and she wasn't looking forward to that tomorrow. As if she didn't have enough to worry about, son number three, Scottie, was having trouble with his teeth. The dentist asked her if he was eating too much junk food. When Liam told her of the events of the evening, she said that at least Tim knew what the UN was. That was something. Plenty of teachers didn't know what the UN was these days. "We have lots to be thankful for," she said.

A week later the Redmonds had one of their big family discussions over dinner. What with sports and the two jobs, these occasions were becoming less frequent as the years went by. Liam asked the boys if they knew the difference between the terms parliament and government and, when it turned out they didn't, went into an elaborate explanation. He was secretly hoping that at least one of them would be attracted to the law, a profession he thought he might have been good at himself, if he'd been given the chance. When the subject got around to sports, Tim said he was going to give up hockey next year. He had been talking to Mr. Breen, who suggested that he take up dramatics or cross-country skiing instead. He hadn't made up his mind which of the two it would be, but the thought of being out in the twilight on the ski trails made him feel good. Mr. Breen himself was going to coach the ski team.

There was a silence after Tim's announcement. Bride gave Liam a glance over the table, and he got the message. Then Scottie, normally a slow eater but not so today because there was a good movie on TV, piped up, "Dad, you forgot to say grace, and I'm just about finished." And so, indeed, he had forgotten. After looking around at the boys who were briefly his, he insisted that everybody lay down the forks and knives right away; and he took his time and said it, changing a word here and there because the meal was more than half over.

Side effects

Rudy Snow had been talking for five minutes at least. Then he paused and looked at his teacup. He examined it, indeed, with such care that someone just joining the group at the table might have thought him a collector who had come upon a specimen of Limoges china in an unlikely spot. There was some hesitant shuffling of chairs. But he started again. "I woke up once in the pitch black," he said. "I thought for a minute I was dead. I was lying on a sofa. In somebody's living room, I guessed. No, not guessed; hoped. Whose, I didn't know. How did I get there? Is that what you're thinking? No idea. Still don't know. My neck was on the arm rest, and was it ever stiff. All my clothes were on, shoes, overcoat, everything. There was no blanket over me. My head was splitting. I was cold. That was how I knew I wasn't in hell, the cold! Brrr!" He shivered to make his point. He was a storyteller who acted out his adventures, winking all the while, his head shaking, arms waving. "In my sleep I'd put my hands between my legs to keep them warm, and when I took them out I got pins and needles. I put out my right hand like this"—he made a flamboyant gesture—"and moved it in a circle all around me. I touched nothing. Nothing there! Then I moved it down, thinking for a second or two there was nothing that way either. But I felt the floor. The sofa was on a floor. At least I had that."

He drank from his cup and looked at the three students. "What happened then?" the one who was smoking asked. He was using a cigarette holder, letting it dangle from his fingers in a delicate manner. "Just a minute," said Rudy. He slid out of the seat and went to the counter to get more sugar. The three friends were in their youth, but Rudy showed the marks of time. He had the stoop of a much older man, his face was pock-marked from some early encounter with disease, and his hairline receded well back. His true age was suggested by his quick movements, for he was thin and jumpy, and by his eyes, which shone with excitement as he talked.

He was back in the booth in a few seconds and stirred in the two lumps. "I won't tell you how I got out of that house, how many ashtrays and God knows what else I knocked over in the dark, or even who owned the house. That's another story." He had a queer, wispy laugh when he thought he had said something funny, a strongly aspirated "Hee, hee, hee!" that sounded like the beginning of a convulsion. Now he laughed a lot, showing rows of brown teeth, some of them broken. "You might know the people. They're still alive."

A sip of tea. Another dash to the counter for two more lumps, his old black raincoat flying.

"But the floor, boys! I thought I'd found something with that floor. I can't tell you how it made me feel. But listen to what I did the day after." Pause. Sip.

"I walked over to my sister's, sat her down at the kitchen table, and asked who my father was. Don't ask me why I did it. Now you don't know this, but I'm an orphan. Reared in Mount Cashel Orphanage, which is why I help out every year with the raffle. But until the age of thirty-five, boys, honest to God, I only knew three things about myself. First, I had a sister, Nellie, married to Jack Mahoney on Colonial Street. Second, my mother died having me. And third, my father's name was Fred Neave. Neave"—he spelled it out—"funny sort of name, not a Newfoundland name, is it? Three things"—he held up a hand with only three fingers on it—"and don't go asking me about my finger now, that's another story. Three things, that's all. Aside from Nellie, I had no relatives in St. John's that I knew about. My mom was an only child from one of the Snow families in the East End, and her mother and father died, oh, fifty, sixty years ago. Died young. Kept to themselves, strange couple; that's what someone told Nellie one time. No, lads, I was left alone in the world with Nellie. And I didn't see a lot of her. You can guess why." He cleaned off a spot on the table with his sleeve.

"Nellie's a year older than me. Was, rest her soul. 'Nellie,' I said to her—you know, the day I went to see her—'Nellie, who's my father?' She knew nothing about him apart from his name, which I already had. He hadn't crossed her mind in twenty years. That's what she told me. 'Don't you know anything? His age? Where he came from? Think hard, Nellie,' I asked her. I didn't mean to push her like that; had no right to, when you come right down to it. I'd given her a bit of trouble from time to time over the years. I don't want to go into that now. Another story there, too. Anyway, she got mad. 'What the hell odds about him?' she said. 'He was a louse, anyway. To leave us like that. Some scummy sailor, that's all he was.' 'How did you find that out?' said I.

'I remember someone saying it when I was a child,' she said. 'Something about his being a sailor who came into St. John's a few times. I can't remember who it was that told me, but she got it from Mom. And that's all I know about him, every scrap.' Well, now, you see, I had something. It wasn't much, but a fact, or what passed for a fact. A thing to stand on, know what I mean?"

The student with the cigarette holder nodded. His companions grunted, waited for more. One was studying Anglo-American diplomacy at the end of the eighteenth century and had made a number of significant discoveries. The other was fast becoming an authority on the Scottish literary renaissance.

"You've got to try to picture it. Before I learned that fact—well, I didn't know who I was. I was thirty-five, as I told you. Not young, you know that. Hope you do, anyway. I had tried it all and done nothing, get the point? After school I went to college to try law, dropped that after a week. Tackled business a couple of times." He now leaned forward as if to make sure that nobody at a nearby table heard him. "That's what I tell youngsters to do when they ask me for advice. Do something yourself, I say, start up a small business, one that people will find useful, don't wait around for someone to pay you a salary. Putting them on the right track, you know the way it is. Not that I was any good at it myself, mind you. Not then, anyway." He laughed again, roared. "Look, I even went into politics. With Social Credit, if you can believe that. Joe Smallwood had the Liberals all sewed up, and I didn't want to go CCF or PC, though my sister was PC. Like a rock, like all the East Enders. Social Credit! Hee, hee, hee! Got nowhere with it, naturally. Didn't understand it first or last. Just tried it. Young then, like you. Later on, I joined up with Joe on the Liberal Reform ticket, but it was too late. Too late for him, even. His day was over. It's hard to tell when your day is over, isn't it? Eh? So I kind of drifted down, as I said, till I hit that floor."

He stopped. An idea struck him. "Boys, how about another cup of tea? They're still serving up there. I'll buy."

But the inquirer into diplomacy went up and bought the tea. He brought back a handful of sugar lumps too. The young men had work to do, but the eye of the storyteller held them.

"So I sized up what I had to do. I knew nothing whatsoever about the merchant marine, the navy, or anything else connected with the salt water. Knew enough to stay away from it, that's all. Nothing about the fishery, either. That's one thing I just hadn't tried, though old Joe was trying to get me into it once. How I was lucky enough to escape it, I'll never know. And I didn't have a clue about how to look things up in books and records. To tell you the truth, I'd never borrowed a book from a library. That's how far behind I was. Fellows like you, you've been at this racket from your teens. You don't know what it's like to start off from nothing when you're halfway along. In life, I mean." For a second he gave them a reproachful look.

"But start off I did. My mom had called him a sailor, and we don't call fishermen sailors around here, so I took it for granted he wasn't a fisherman coming in on a trawler from some outharbour. And St. John's girls wouldn't mess with baymen in those days, not like now. Besides, as I told you, it wasn't a local name. Then I took a chance and cut the merchant marine. He'd been here in the war years, and I guessed with the navy. Now the merchant marine was back and forth here during the war too, but there were more navy men about and I figured they were younger and more after the women. A man in the Archives said that was where he'd look if he was me. Anyway, I started with the navies: the Canadian first, then the British. Oh, those Admiralty lists! How many thousands of names did I read, I wonder? And letters going all over the place!" His arms flew. "I got to be a bit of an expert on St. John's harbour in the war, what ships came in, where they docked, what they were doing here. I don't suppose there's a man alive who knows more than I do about all that. What was the biggest ship to come through the Narrows in World War Two? You're smart fellows, answer me that."

No response.

He sniffed in triumph. "Well, I guarantee you that I know. Yes, and the second biggest, and the third. See the kind of stuff I got in my head? A lot of it useless, not like what's in yours. You don't know the half of it. I was looking through lists in the Archives and the old newspapers every spare minute I could get away from my job. I was selling insurance at the time, but not doing much with it. But I wasn't, you know"—he lifted the cup—"at that, anyway. I found all the looking hard on my eyes and had to get a loan of my sister's glasses. She wasn't using them much at that point. After a few weeks I started to like it. The work, I mean. I started to enjoy going off on tangents, looking into things in the papers that sometimes had nothing to do with the war: how many were contracting TB, what the fishery was like, things like that. That's the killer. Here I was, working alongside people like you—scholars, gentlemen—and enjoying it. Every minute of it." Big laugh.

"You're not wearing glasses now," said the renaissance scholar.

"Got contacts now, Mr. man. Right up to date. Rubber ones. You want to see one? No trouble to pop one out here on the table. All right, another time. I have a few dollars. Now, I mean. I don't mind saying it. I thought I'd try something different. Why shouldn't I have contacts, as well as the next man? Tell me that. Not everybody wants to look at a man with glasses."

The tea was gone again, and there was no hope of getting more. He looked down in the cup as if in disbelief, then turned it upside down in the saucer and considered it from another angle. What was it? Sèvres, perhaps? Dresden?

The sugar that had liquefied in the bottom of the cup trickled into the saucer, and he scraped it up with a finger of his maimed hand and licked it off.

"The upshot? I couldn't find him on the Canadian or British lists. That left the Americans. My letters to Washington—I wrote about five of them—got the answer, no. No Frederick Neave in the US Navy. I tried the other services too, just in case. No. I went back and tried the RAF and British Army, and the RCAF and Canadian Army. No all round. Time was going by, you understand? In the middle of all this, Nellie died. Leukemia. I had to help bury her. You know, money. I was solo now for sure." Mournful look, pause. "I was beginning to think that life wasn't fair. Could you blame me? Could you?"

His spoon fell off the table. No one stirred.

"I was about to try the merchant marine, which I knew was going to be very hard work, when one day I met an American whose name was Manfred Blair. He walked in off the street wanting to buy insurance, if you can believe that. First and last time that happened to me. So I sold him a policy and wrote to Washington again, and sure enough got a letter back saying that Manfred Neave had served in the US Navy and had been in the North Atlantic theatre of war, including St. John's. This had to be him. The years matched, and to tell you the truth he was the only Neave I ever heard of, in or out of the services, who had set foot in St. John's during the war. Lots of Neales, some Nearys, couple of Neatbys, but no Neaves. Just to make sure I went through some of the lists again, and wrote off to Ottawa and London to see if any Neaves—see, I forgot Wilfred too—were on any of their lists of people connected with the war in Newfoundland. I don't know how much checking they did, but the answers were no. This was him, lads. No question." He gave a big smile, then frowned.

"Was I happy? That what you're asking? Wait till you hear what else was in the letter. He enlisted in New York, the

Navy told me, and gave his permanent address as a hotel in Manhattan. So I still didn't know where he came from. Under Next of Kin he'd written "None." When he signed up in 1939 he was twenty-four, five feet ten inches tall, a hundred and thirty pounds—thin as a rake, apparently—and in good health. You know who he was like? Like me, that's who. I couldn't believe it. There was just one thing more in the letter. Manfred Neave was declared missing in action and presumed dead, in the Battle of Tassafaronga near Guadalcanal, on November 30, 1943."

The listeners stirred, moved cups and saucers.

"Oh no, I wasn't finished. Still had one or two tricks up my sleeve. There was nothing that was going to bowl me over, let me tell you. Not after all I'd been through. I wrote a letter to the American embassy in Tokyo and asked about prisoner of war camps over there. You mightn't know this, but the Japanese had prisoners of war too, and not just in Burma and places like that. They took some back to Japan. And looked after them, I won't say how well. They kept records too. Yes, sir. Was there a Manfred Neave on the Japanese POW lists? That's what I wanted to know. It was just about the last straw, you have to see that. What was left of his bones was almost certainly in the Pacific near the Solomon Islands. I knew. I'm no fool. But I was really caught up in this now, and had to go to the bitter end. See my point?"

The diplomat saw and nodded.

"A month later, on the same day mind, I got two letters, one from Japan and another from Washington. The state this time, not DC. The first one told me that Manfred Neave died of pneumonia in a POW camp in Hokkaido, Japan, in June, 1945, and was buried there in a graveyard reserved for Americans. They gave me the exact address. I have it at home. It was a marked grave, and I was welcome to visit it if I wished. The second letter was from a woman in Olympia who had been referred to me by the Department of the Navy. She had written the Navy a number of times to ask about troops stationed in Newfoundland during the war, and finally a secretary sent her a note saying that I might be able to help. The secretary must have remembered getting those letters from me about my dad. As it happened, I could answer the questions, and I did. The woman sent me a check for one hundred dollars. American." He stopped talking, cleared his throat.

"I haven't been over to Japan yet, my lads. Might never go, you know how life is, the way time slips by. I hope you do, anyway. But the thing is, I could go there tomorrow and put my hand down on his grave if I wanted to." He looked at his hands and muttered something inaudible.

"I've thought about him a lot since I got the last letter. I went looking for him, but it wasn't him I found. He's like a shadow. There was so little trace of a personality that it seems he hardly touched the earth. Yet touch it he did. The visible signs? Passion repeated, two orphans, two deaths. My pain, too. Isn't that a lot? Try to answer that. I think, yes. You can't hide. Bound to be side effects, breakage. Agree?"

Nods. A bell sounded in the front hall over their heads. Women were cleaning off the tables.

"Now we come to the funny part. He ran away, right? To hell with us, right? But he did me a lot of good. You see, what I did was this. I gave up the insurance business as soon as I got the hundred dollars from Washington. I never made easy money like that before. What, a hundred bucks for digging around a few hours in the Archives or a library, and then writing a paragraph or two! Once I got the money I made up a card describing myself as a researcher—bold as brass, my buckoes—and put an ad here and there in the American papers. Can't tell you which ones. Trade secret. I've been making a good living ever since. Got a few contacts upstairs, too"—he pointed with his thumb—"it all helps. Add it together, I've got a dollar or two. And I wouldn't have made it without my father, because I wouldn't know where to look for stuff if I hadn't looked him up. So it's queer, isn't it? Turned out to be fair after all, in a way. Eh? Life, I mean?"

More nods. Rudy started out of the booth and said they'd better go up and clear off their desks before the place closed. As he slid out, he picked the spoon up off the floor.

"That story..." said the boy who smoked.

Rudy knew this young fellow wanted to be a writer. "Now, Gus," he said, standing by the table. "I shouldn't have told you that story. You'll go and write that up. I want to write it up myself one of these days, please God. When I get to be as good at it as you fellows. Tell you what, if I pop off, you can have it. No chance of that for a spell, I hope. I'm only forty-seven."

The three friends could see him touch wood in five or six places as he bounced up the stairs chuckling to himself, with the old raincoat billowing behind him.

Bus ride

The crowded No. 7 bus was stuck in the late afternoon traffic in Oxford Street. Looking towards Marble Arch, Dermot Kennedy could see the line of overhanging, triangular Christmas lights that had been officially switched on by the Duchess of York a few weeks before. These were set off on either side of the street by a long row of flickering lights attached to the leafless trees. On the corner of Berners Street, away from the glare of the shop windows and traffic lights, he could make out the orange embers of a chestnut vendor's fire vanishing and reappearing as shoppers hurried by, like a star behind scudding clouds.

Pedestrians crossed the street in front of the bus, their breath turning to mist in the cold air and mingling with the fumes from cars and lorries. Cabbies who had picked the wrong way to their destinations lost their fares and tried to edge out of traffic and make an escape through Soho. The bus's diesel rumbled. The street was full of noises, people shouting and horns blowing. Two lovers went by, quarreling. They got close enough to the bus for Dermot to see that the man was weeping. A policeman trotted by on horseback, edging his way in and out of traffic. Against all odds, the horse seemed to be making a comeback in London.

Dermot could have gone home on the underground, but there was no reason to rush. The bus would take him there in due course. He liked the atmosphere of a London double-decker; the noise, drama, bustle. He enjoyed the experience of solitude in the middle of a crowd, the role of outsider. The ride also gave him time to mull things over.

"And she only thirty-three," a red-haired woman sitting next to him was saying to her blonde companion across the aisle. Dermot had chosen the downstairs front seat, to the left of the driver's caboose. This gave him a clear view of the street in front of the bus, and at the same time the reflection in the glass showed what was happening in the seats behind. It was a strategic location. It was better on top, of course, but the front seats up there were usually taken, often by hostile youngsters.

The two women had got on at Tottenham Court Road station, loaded down with parcels. They were young—early to mid-twenties, he thought—and very pretty. Secretaries? Too many rings. More likely housewives, in from Reading or Rugby for the day, returning with their booty.

"'So what if he up and left?' I said to her." The redhead had a gentle voice. "'It's a pity, but what can be done about it?' But she didn't see things my way. Although she told me her mother said the same things to her that I said. So it's not as if nobody is giving her good advice. People won't take advice these days, will they?"

"And she with the job she has," said the blonde, whose voice was soft, too.

"I know," returned the redhead. "Hard to believe, isn't it? She's more than an operator now, did you know that? Oh yes, she sets up computer programs for the company. She gets four hundred quid a week, she told me, company car, perks. Travels all the time—Birmingham, Falmouth, Edinburgh. She went to Malta last summer. Imagine! Stays in five-star hotels. Then there's the beaches. When you think about the opportunities she has, not just to get ahead but to go to parties, meet people—nice people—you start to wonder. I feel sorry for her, but I wish I had her chances."

"It's over a year now, isn't it?"

"Year and a half, more like. He's gone for good, I'd say. Wouldn't you? Everybody says there's no hope. He's taken up with someone else, anyway, more suited to his way of thinking, I hear. He wanted, you know, an ordinary wife. A lot to be said for it, if you ask me. Not that I have much time for him, mind you. I don't. But someone's got to look after the domestic side. I always felt that. It doesn't pay to have help these days."

The bus lurched ahead about twenty feet, and the West Indian conductor came through the aisle collecting fares. The two women paid their way to Paddington. Another conversation, about the prices paid for antique furniture at Christie's auction house, was in progress behind Dermot's back. An old man, about halfway down the bus, had commenced shouting "Nazi!" every two or three minutes to people walking outside.

"Pay no attention to dat chap. He sees dem everywhere," said the conductor while spinning off tickets and giving change to the women. They smiled and fell silent. The conductor turned, raised his hand, and announced that gangs of pickpockets were at work along Oxford Street at this time of year. He advised all passengers to keep a careful watch on their handbags and parcels. A woman had lost money in the bus yesterday. He didn't like to hear of it happening at all, but certainly not in his bus. It wasn't good for his reputation. "Stop your yellin', mon," he said to the Nazi-hunter on his way down the aisle. "You're disturbin' de passengers." But before long the old fellow resumed his scrutiny of passers-by. Dermot saw that two rough-looking, skinhead types got in the bus and sat near him, but even that didn't prevent his occasional shouts. Identification of the enemy was to him a matter of urgency.

"So what's she going to do?" asked the blonde.

"That's just it, isn't it?" said the redhead. "What is she going to do with herself? I've no idea, and I don't think she has either. They've no kiddies, so all she has at night when she goes home is her work and her flat. She takes a bushel of files home with her all the time. The manager is starting to ask her advice about appointments in the company. That's how high up she is. But she hasn't much of a life, if you ask me. I invited her to come for a meal a couple of times, but it's a long journey just to have supper and it's not safe going back alone late at night. She won't stay over or come on weekends, in case he calls. That's what she says. He'll never call her now, of course, after the latest."

"She sounds really unhappy."

"Well, she is. I lose patience with her a bit, to tell you the truth. When you think of all she has. And she's a diamond, a proper diamond. But she thinks she's missed the boat somehow. With him, I mean. Says if she'd only tried harder, given in to him more, it might've been different. She didn't realize how strong he felt until it was too late, apparently. She's worried about losing what's really important, so she says. Thirty-three's not young for a woman."

"Nazi!" shouted the old man, pointing to an Aryan type crossing the street on a green light. He could spot Germans, all right, Dermot thought. The bus was moving slowly past Selfridges department store, with its window displays of elaborate Yuletide scenes. "Joy to the World" could be heard somewhere in the distance. Dermot was being nudged by parcels. He was warm. One of the toughs near the old man had lit a cigarette, though there was supposed to be no smoking downstairs.

The redhead continued: "She started to cry a fortnight ago when I was with her. Honest. You wouldn't think it to look at her, she's so cool. But she did. 'I blew it, I think, Liz,' she said. She'd just heard he took up with the other woman. I had to comfort her. 'There's dozens out there, Rachel,' I said. 'Better than him, ten times better. Open your eyes.' 'Did I want the wrong things?' she asked me. What could I say? I mean, in the circumstances. So I said, 'No, you didn't. Everybody's after what you got, girl. Thousands'd change places with you.' I did my best to cheer her up. No good. Damn his eyes, I say. I wish to hell she'd never seen him. Did I tell you he tried to get fresh with me at a party once?"

"No!"

"He did, then. About three years ago. Hand up my knickers. Wanted to teach me a thing or two about living, he said. You had to grab it when you could: that was his opinion. Always did have one thing on his mind, as far as I could see. She may be better off, eventually."

"You passed him up, with his looks?"

"I did. Hubby was at the party, just to give one reason. But I tried to think of her, too."

"What are you doing tonight?" asked the blonde.

"I thought I'd pop back into town to see her. Maybe bring her some chocolate. She's always had a taste for soft centers. She's in the Middlesex, but I'm sure it's only for a week or two. She told the company she wanted a holiday. Overwork, she said."

The blonde now searched through one of her bags. "I've some of that new Paris perfume here somewhere," she said. "Let's be devils and put some on before we get on the train."

Dermot got up, fought his way through the parcels, and pulled the string for the request stop. "Nazi!" the man hissed at him as he walked towards the rear. He stopped, but the two skinheads looked sourly at him. "You want trouble, mate?" one asked. "He's our uncle," said the other. "We sort of keep an eye on him." They both grinned at this. Dermot moved on, tripping over something and almost falling on his face.

The bus pulled in to the curb and he got off. He was on Praed Street, a few stops before his usual one. He watched carefully as the bus pulled away. Much to his relief, the skinheads stayed on board. A ten-minute walk before his dinner was just what he needed. Perhaps he'd have some mulled wine too when he got home, for the chill. It was the season for such things. He set off quickly for the next street lamp about a hundred yards away. It was a little risky to be walking on poorly lit streets, even at this hour.

Middle son

Jimmy Byrne had chums, but he knew from early childhood that his real friend, the one he could always look to for a helping hand, was his brother Colin. Although Colin was a year older, they were in the same grade at school, two behind Alphonsus. The eldest was headed for great things. For years money had been set aside for his education. He was to go to St. Bon's College in St. John's, then on to university in Canada to train as a lawyer. Their Aunt Aggie, a spinster nurse who visited Long Beach from time to time to keep an eye on her aged mother living with the Byrnes, offered to support this aim, which had been first defined when

Alphonsus was ten or eleven. From then on, legal ambition was to be the centre of the family's life. A Long Beach Byrne a lawyer! That was something worth scrimping for. Well known to have plenty of brains, Alphonsus stuck to his books and led his class throughout his school years. Destiny awaited him.

Coming up behind, Jimmy and Colin weren't exactly neglected, though what was to be done with them hadn't been worked out. No money had been put aside for them, that was clear. There was only so much to go around. Paddy Byrne was a fisherman and times were hard. "Long Beach's day is over," he'd say when he dragged back from hauling trawls on the offshore banks; and his wife Molly, who came from what she regarded as a more respectable place up the shore, Northern Bay, agreed. She encouraged Paddy to leave fishing altogether to go to work in the mines in New Waterford up in Nova Scotia. One of her sisters lived there and was doing well. "Anywhere at all will do," she said, "but for God's sake get me out of this hole." And he did try the mines, the docks in Halifax, a labourer's job on the new airport in Gander, and carpenter work in St. John's. But he always left his wife and children behind, and then, after getting a bit of money together, came back to fishing. "Back to misery," she'd say bitterly. He was a very good fisherman, as he had to be to feed a growing family in Long Beach. After Jimmy there was a gap of some years, but then came three daughters in quick succession. When his youngest sister, Janey, started walking, Jimmy saw his father smash the cradle to pieces over the cabbage-garden fence, an action which the passing of time would reveal to be premature.

With Alphonsus growing into his teens and starting to chase the girls, their father away from home or consumed with fishing and other toil, and their mother looking after babies, once they did their chores Jimmy and Colin were mostly left to themselves. They played together and competed with one another in and out of school. Though young for his grade, Jimmy was a whiz at Arithmetic and English, and often ended up ahead of Colin in the class. Tom Johnson, a trucker's son from Northern Bay, would come first, Jimmy second, Colin third or fourth. Jimmy was skinny, sickly, and had poor teeth. The teachers made a pet out of him, and he would get to give recitations at the school concerts or make presentations to visitors. One summer he was picked to present a scroll to Governor Macdonald, who was making his farewell tour of the island. "I know he's sorry to be leaving," Molly said. "No mistake about it."

Colin's talents were less apparent. He was good at drawing, science, and history, but "slow to middling" in other subjects, as one teacher wrote on his report card. And this was the prevailing view. Normally subdued and retiring, he was somewhat more robust than Jimmy and would take his brother's part in the fist fights that broke out in the school yard. What made him formidable in these encounters was less his strength, for he too was thin and pale, than his savage temper when roused. "He's a deep one," Jimmy heard one of the teachers remark of Colin who, when asked one day in class what Newfoundland's main industry was, answered "American bases." Everyone else in the room knew it was the fishery or pulp and paper. It had to be one or the other.

Another day the class was asked to write on "The happiest day of my life." All the pupils knew the day in question was the one they had received their First Holy Communion. All except Colin, who wrote on "The Day a Black Bear chased me in the Woods." Jimmy didn't know what to make of that, because he and Colin picked berries together and went trouting in the brooks and ponds all the time, and no bear had ever chased them. If Colin had seen one when he was wandering on his own, he would have mentioned it when he came home. But he hadn't. There were no bears, black or brown, in the Byrne family history. When Colin started reading out his composition, Jimmy turned around and stared at him. But he was smiling and chuckling softly as he read it. Nobody said a word until the story of the bear was over. Then the teacher had a lot to say about the importance of telling the truth. Colin said nothing. "It was a hard topic to write on," he told Jimmy later. It was queer to hear his voice in class because he sat in the back and most of the time didn't answer questions. The few answers he gave were humdingers.

There was a chirping one day in class, and the teacher found a bird in Colin's pocket. When he was questioned, he said he found it in the grove behind the school during recess. "His wing is broke," he said, "and the cats'll eat him if I don't take him home." But the teacher was mad and made him take the bird back to the grove. The teacher was new to the school. He came from Lourdes, somewhere on the west coast of the island. He once pulled Colin's ear so hard he made it bleed. "Lourdes must be out in the uncivilized part of Newfoundland," Molly said when she saw what had happened.

One fine summer's day when he was eleven, Colin disappeared. He didn't go only for an hour or two, in the manner of most youngsters who duck their chores. It wasn't like him to err in a conventional way; an impulse towards the extreme was in his character. And so in the evening, when the family assembled for a supper of bologna and beans, they discovered that Colin was absent and hadn't been seen since early morning. His trouting pole was in its usual place in the cellar. A search was started. First they looked into the well, then the nearby groves, gullies, and swimming holes. There was no sign of him. No neighbour had seen him all day. "He's so quiet, I hardly take notice of him," one woman said. "One minute he's there, the next he's gone." And it was true that there was a shadowy quality about him that invited overlooking; yet the future would show he was real enough, blood and bone.

Long Beach was now in an uproar. Jimmy's sisters were scared and upset, because Colin was a favourite who watched over them tenderly, keeping them away from cliffs, horses, and other dangers. A big planning session with the neighbours was in progress around the kitchen table when the oldest girl, Elizabeth, went and looked behind the porch door that had been left open all day because of the heat, and there was Colin, standing where he had been for hours, grinning, silent. "Sweet hand of Jesus," Paddy Byrne said; but he didn't give him a licking or even send him to bed without his supper because of the fright everybody got. "That little Christer'll be the death of me yet," he added. For a few years the Byrnes turned the incident into a family joke. "You going out in the porch to spend the night?" someone would ask Colin around bedtime; or, if his looks came up for comment, as they sometimes did when the family realized how little interest he had in girls, somebody might say, "His nose was flattened out behind the porch door."

While Colin may never have been chased by a bear, he spent a lot of time, often by himself, in the woods and marshlands that stretched for miles to the north and west behind Long Beach. An expert berry picker, he knew where all the best spots were, far inland on the barrens. There was something in this wild, bleak, empty stretch of barren ground, Jimmy would say later when this came up for discussion, that touched a chord in Colin's spirit; the rocky paths, rough underfoot and overgrown with nettles and alders, offered a kind of freedom. By the time they reached high school, the two explorers had a collection of quartz crystals and other minerals. They would spend evenings scrambling over tolts and glacial debris in search of specimens, taking time out to enjoy foundering cliffs, pretending they were Frank and Joe Hardy. Colin also found an abandoned ochre pit under a cliff that called for investigation. A huge chunk of granite called Peg's Rock a mile inland on the ridge behind Long Beach was a favoured spot for playing. Not everyone could climb Peg's Rock because the handholds were so small. Colin and Jimmy would sometimes stand on it on sunny days and shout things in the direction of the salt water, a wide expanse across which could be seen the blue shape of Cape St. Francis. Behind the cape, they knew, lay St. John's. "I'm getting out of that hole," Colin yelled one day from the rock as he looked towards Long Beach. "I'm going to study geology." He later quietly announced this intention at the kitchen table, where it was not encouraged. "To go to work in a bank would be nice," said their mother. Jimmy knew Colin hated adding up figures and was no good at writing things out. He couldn't even do his ovals right when he started school, and learning the McLean Method had little beneficial effect on his crabbed handwriting.

In grade nine, Tom Johnson again came first, Jimmy second, and Colin third, continuing what was now an established pattern. This was a year of growing seriousness in the school. Although the Gull Islanders, a tough crowd from the next outport down the shore, went on debating whether Hank Snow or Wilf Carter was the better singer, the pupils from Northern Bay were considering what they were going to be when they grew up. Tom Johnson decided he was cut out to be an engineer. "No sooner said than done," Molly said. "John and Mag Johnson got the cash. You can make piles of money if you own a truck." The Johnsons didn't just own a truck. They had a car too, and drove down to Long Beach to go to mass on Sunday mornings, picking up a couple of people extra along the way if it was raining. Jimmy and Colin would watch them park by the paling fence in front of the church and then stroll up to the front steps. Someone said the fence had been "painted brown to match the mud."

In grade nine, Tom Johnson also won the $5 prize in a school essay contest on "How to make Improvements on the North Shore." The parish priest suggested the subject; he wanted to make sure his part of Conception Bay benefited from the coming of Confederation. "If you come up with good ideas, I'll get the money to start them," he said over the altar. The priest had good contacts with the member for the district, and with the Crosbies and Pippys in St. John's. The winning entry was on "The Importance of Henneries." Jimmy entered the contest too, writing, at his mother's suggestion, on "Carrying Freight to St. John's and Other Places." His essay didn't place in the top three; nor did Colin's on "Minerals in this Area," in which he enlarged on the advantages offered by iron ore, ochre, and peat moss. Their father read the two essays when the contest was over and said it was fine and dandy to talk of carrying freight to St. John's, but what kind of freight was it going to be? The fishery was just about dead, and you didn't need many trucks for the few poor miserable berries in the fall. As for Colin's idea, he said he didn't think peat moss was a mineral. "There's nothing worth talking about underground here," he added.

In the summer after grade nine, their mother had a bad spell, and for a few weeks a woman from Gull Island came to look after the Byrne children. By September, Molly was back on her feet in time to get Alphonsus ready to go to St. Bon's, where he was to be a boarding student for a year before going off to university on the mainland. His letters home were eagerly awaited by the whole family. Jimmy and Colin got to know the names of all the students in his class and became devoted fans of the St. Bon's hockey and basketball teams. St. Bon's dominated the family discussions. When Alphonsus came back at Christmas—a grim one in which Colin got a pen and Jimmy a geometry set—he looked grown up in his blazer, blue and gold tie, and white shirt.

Their mother decided that it was to be a big year for the younger boys too. "This is the key grade, grade ten," she said. "If you do well in that, grade eleven is easy." She made a rule that Jimmy and Colin were to study at the kitchen table every weeknight for two hours, a severe discipline which they alleviated by hiding *Kidnapped* and *Lost Endeavour* inside their big geography books. She also decided that this was the year to send out application forms. "It's about time we won something in this house," she said. She herself made application only to the Sodality of the Little Flower, but Jimmy and Colin applied for Imperial Oil scholarships even though preference was given to "children of employees of Imperial Oil," and for Canadian Legion bursaries though they weren't "children or dependents of a war veteran." Molly said: "What odds? Apply anyway. They may have a bit of money left over when they get finished with their own." A form wasn't needed for the really big scholarship, the electoral, but nobody on the whole shore had ever won one of those, as far as they knew. In the meantime, at school Tom Johnson maintained his prominence, so quick was he at the two math subjects and General Science. Jimmy and most of the other pupils were having trouble with Algebra.

Before the year ended, Jimmy came down with scarlet fever and mumps, complicated by toothache, and had to spend two weeks in bed. During exam week he had headaches and vomiting, and in the last test, Algebra, which some students finished in less than an hour, he got two problems wrong, found his mistakes with ten minutes left, and had to keep writing up to the last minute to correct them. He blotted his exam book in two places as he finished, making the blots worse by trying to rub them out. He said little to his mother when he got home.

The summer passed in gloom and anxiety. A province-wide polio scare kept all the Byrne family close to home, except Alphonsus, who had joined the army cadets in St. Bon's and was off at camp in Nova Scotia. His letters explained how hard the military life was, but he left no doubt where he preferred to be. Everybody missed him. The fishery was poor again. In August they could see that blueberries were going to be scarce, a serious matter since that was where the money came from for school books. Nevertheless, Jimmy and Colin tackled the berries as soon as the season opened, going far into the barrens with their wooden boxes strapped to their backs and returning late in the afternoon, their shoulders stiff and sore from the long haul. In late August, after a gruelling, hot day, they came over the ridge near Peg's Rock with their heavy boxes and sat on the rock to take a spell. As usual, Colin had picked eight gallons, Jimmy about four and a half. Colin lingered on top of the rock, yelling and singing, watching birds circle far overhead. It was a good feeling to be almost home when your box was full.

As they headed down the hill, they spotted their sisters coming up the path towards them. What was this about? Did someone in Long Beach have polio? Had Aunt Aggie turned up? Was the baby sick? The girls were running hard. Halfway down the path, Jimmy looked over his shoulder to see if someone else, their grandmother maybe, somebody worth all the running, was coming behind them. But there wasn't. At last Elizabeth and the second oldest, Lucy, reached the two tired pickers, with Janey trailing well behind. It took a few seconds for them to catch their breath. "Scholarship!" Lucy shouted at last, "Jimmy got the electoral scholarship!" "A hundred dollars!" gasped Elizabeth. Janey now entered the picture and clung to his leg in her happiness. All three danced around him as he made the hero's walk home. "You got ninety-nine in Algebra," Lucy said.

The next day Colin didn't go in the woods and, in fact, was nowhere to be seen when Jimmy left early in the morning. When he got back, well past suppertime and with only three gallons, Colin picked a fight with him for no reason, and threatened to hit him with the hammer. Their mother and father had dressed up to the nines and gone up the shore visiting, Lucy told him, so Jimmy had to fight back. After taking a couple of hard knocks, he pinned Colin to the ground and held his arms down in the grass. This astonished him. Colin wasn't strong at all! He could be whipped. "Say uncle," Jimmy said, demanding the usual formula of surrender. No word or nod came back. This called for harder action. Jimmy drove Colin's right hand down into the grass and knelt on it in preparation for the Second Deadly Punishment, hair pulling. Colin was crying, but didn't scream when he did this, even though a piece of broken glass, unseen by Jimmy, lay hidden in the grass under his hand and cut deep into the flesh and tendons. Jimmy felt it in his knee and got up right away. As he moved, Colin struck him hard with the wounded hand, driving blood that would not easily come off all over his face and hair. "I don't care," Colin said, looking at the cut. And then, in a dreadful premonition of what would be, "I don't care if I live or die."

Return to laughter

It was more than just the Monday morning blues Jane Shallow felt or the effects of the bleak, cold November day. Her problem was really starting to get her down, and with exam week just around the corner it wasn't easy to get a minute to herself to think about it. It was no good to go home on her free period. That was the source of her trouble. So, when the eleven o'clock bell went, she put on her overcoat and drove to Mamma Trossi's on Churchill Square. If she stayed in the school, she'd have to talk to somebody in the staff room: the principal, Mr. Shannahan, maybe, who had been looking her up and down for some time, sensing she was vulnerable, watching for an opening; or the other English teacher, the dreaded Miss Farmer, whose period off on Mondays Jane knew from sad experience was the same as her own.

Miss Farmer was a chubby, enthusiastic B.A. Honours graduate, fresh out of university, full of ideas about Shakespeare, and determined to make friends. To that end she had joined half the voluntary organizations in St. John's, including the Legion of Mary and, some said, the Liberal Party. "I have an idea about act two!" she'd say as she strode up to a victim in the staff room, *King Lear* in hand and her mouth in full flight. This was the first year the play had been taught in the school, and everybody found it hard. Many of Miss Farmer's notions about it were so far out that they could only have come from some of the cuckoos at the university, but it had to be conceded that now and then she hit the mark. Her students could be heard arguing about the play in the corridors. Mr. Shannahan had to break up one of the arguments because he thought it might get violent.

A favourite with the students after only a few months on staff, Miss Farmer cut no ice with the other teachers. Even Jane, not normally given to malice, once said that you only had to look at her to see what "looped and windowed raggedness" was like. She had a coating of fine hair on her chin and neck, and this, too, gave rise to comment. In fact, it gave Jane the willies. The religion teacher, Mr. Vaughan, was especially good on the hair. "Has she bearded you this morning?" he would say to Jane. Or, brushing by Miss Farmer in the corridor, he might say, "My, that was a close shave." She also had a small mouth, a nose that curved in such a way that it reminded Jane of a puffin's beak, and pale, blotchy skin. It wasn't going to be easy for her to get a man, but the campaign had started.

Mamma Trossi's was one of Jane's special places. When she entered, not a single booth was occupied, so she chose the one in the corner farthest from the door and spread a few papers around to look busy in case someone she knew came in. She ordered coffee and toast and put her feet up, comforted by the thought that she didn't have to be back in school until one o'clock, when the kids returned from lunch. The manager of the restaurant was sweet on her and didn't care how long she lingered over her coffee. She was a regular, ever since the courting days with Frank more than ten years ago. They used to come in after a late movie once a week with friends to drink wine and gorge themselves on pasta or cake, dragging the evening out as long as possible, hating to go home. Some weeks they'd be in two or three times. They had a gang then. Life was fun.

Frank was her problem. She was thinking of leaving him. Correction: had been thinking of it for six months. Why she hadn't been able to walk out on him when the thought first struck her was a mystery. Marriages were breaking up all the time, even in dull old St. John's. It was still a free country. There were no children to worry about. And nobody would notice. Sure, her mom and dad would be upset for a week or so, and a few inquiries would be made at the school and perhaps at a couple of places around town. It would be a ten-day wonder. Half the people she knew were divorced. A girl she had gone to school with, Kathy Horan, got hers two years ago and was living it up in the downtown clubs. Last New Year's Eve someone had seen her dancing on a table at the Sunset Strip, with a bunch of sailors off a Canadian frigate standing around clapping and singing. Meanwhile, Jane was home by herself having a hot toddy before going to bed. Kathy was Jane's age: thirty-seven.

Jane knew that to delay much longer would be fatal. Who looked at a woman over forty these days? She was slim, attractive. There wasn't a gray hair on her head and, thanks to careful attention over the years, her face had no deep lines. She was what men used to call a fine figure of a woman. A bit small in front, she had thought once or twice about an augmentation. Her clothes were expensive. There was a touch of class about her. She knew what she was. And what Frank was. He was a failure. Correction: a drunken failure. A teacher, too, he had long ago given up any interest in his job as a phys-ed instructor, and spent most evenings in the beer tavern with cronies, often staggering home at ten or eleven o'clock at night. Then he'd stink up her kitchen with pizza or fried chicken and fall asleep in front of the TV with some stupid game on from the sports channel.

How the hell had this happened to her? She was the best-looking of all the girls in her high school class. Brainiest too, with maybe one exception. Yet she ended up with the loser, while her pals were driving around in BMWs and going to Hawaii or Gozo for Christmas. One of her school chums, a girl who in her teens was afflicted with acne and cold sores, now lived in a house with about ten bathrooms. Jane and Frank had never been invited into it.

Looking back, it was hard to explain what had happened to him, it was so fast, so pointless. She couldn't find any cause for it apart from his own weakness. Perhaps he was too fond of the company of his buddies, like engineers and hockey players who refused to grow up and spent their thirties and forties patting one another on the bum. Perhaps she should have seen earlier than she did how quickly alcohol was hooking him. But when she came to look, he was gone. Vows of abstinence were extracted but almost immediately broken. She would find flasks under the car seat or behind the garage door. The climax came last June when she came back late from the usual end of term party to find him in her bedroom, totally bombed, sleeping in his street clothes on her new duvet, snoring, drooling, moaning. And the vomity stench of his breath! The scene so disgusted her that she went into the spare room to sleep, and stayed away from her own bed for a week. There had been sex only three times since, at his insistence. She went along with it only because he might find someone in a dirty tavern and bring disease into the house. She just lay there and let him do it.

Whatever he wanted, which wasn't much. She remembered thinking: I've got to give it up some day, so why not now? Who needed sex, anyway?

Correction: she needed it, that's who. She had been faithful for a decade, despite offers from a dozen or so very appealing men. She still got good offers. The truth was, she needed a man...not just a man, a certain kind of man. If one could be found. She was lonely. Having always prided herself on facing facts, she admitted that celibacy was not for her. A sense of missing out on what mattered in life swept over her. There must be more out there somewhere, she thought, there had to be something better than what she had.

In the past few weeks she'd started receiving flowers and other gifts at the school from a man who was working at a printing office. He even phoned her twice, which Mr. Shannahan didn't care for, and once he sent a package by special delivery with only a postcard of Vancouver in it and a note: "This is where I'd like to take you." His insistence made an impression. She checked him out and learned he was younger than she was. But who'd notice? Who noticed anything, nowadays? Personal happiness was all that counted. The world had changed. You had to look out for number one. In her bitter exchanges with Frank she tried to tell him this. "You're a lousy, slobbery drunk," she said to him only a few nights ago. "People have no pity for someone like you, you turkey. Don't expect it, from me or anyone else. There's none for you. You're a reject, a discard, a fool." She had still other words, worse than these. They hurt him, but who cared? They had hardly any friends left in common. Even some of their oldest connections had dropped away once they saw Frank in his cups. Who could blame them? She could get sick when she thought of what he had been in the early days, striding around the house in his jockey shorts on Sunday mornings, getting her breakfast before giving her what he called "the treatment." She could do with some treatment now and, by God, she'd have it.

So what held her back? What was wrong with her? She took her notebook out of her bag and made the usual columns "for" and "against" leaving, putting the word that hadn't passed her lips in six months, and that even now she was half afraid to write down, at the top of the "for" list. As she added other words, noise from a nearby table drew her out of herself. Three men, at the tipsy stage even at this early hour, were eating lasagna and laughing. They were unshaven and dirty, off a trawler, perhaps, or fresh out of the lumberwoods. Or truckers, they could be that. The ringleader was insisting that the common rosé wine he had ordered should be wrapped in a cloth napkin and properly poured by a waiter and, furthermore, that it be sampled before serving. He tasted a small portion three or four times. "It's not a good wine," he said, smacking his lips. "Slightly tart, vinegary. Must have been a bad year." He smelled it, sticking his nose far down the glass. "No bouquet either," he went on. "On a scale of one to ten, I'd give it, oh, three and a half." He burped, then said he was tempted to send it back to the wine cellar. But, looking grimly at his companions, who might have been slightly more under the weather than he was, he concluded that "It's good enough for these two. Let's have it." The waiter poured, and all three drank. "Would madam care for a sip?" asked the main drinker, noting that Jane was taking an interest in their proceedings. The others guffawed, and she looked away.

A loathing of all men surged up in her, a longing to escape for good from their hairiness, vile odours, secretions, grunts, fondling their John Thomases, the lot. Down from the waist, they weren't so pretty either. She shook her head and went back to her brooding. Did she want a man at all? For a moment she had her doubts. At least she knew what Frank's habits were. But to get used to somebody else's problems could be just as appalling. Her printer might have psoriasis or hemorrhoids for all she knew, or something even more ghastly. Not to speak of bizarre sexual needs, to be disclosed, perhaps, the night after the knot was tied when he came out of the bathroom in a negligee and garter belt with a blue ribbon tied around his thing. What would she be expected to do then, in God's name? The prospect of getting to know another set of relatives also made her weary. She had enough hooks in her. More uncles and cousins she didn't need.

Some others started drifting into the restaurant for lunch. Nobody who knew her, thank God. She chewed her toast and drank the cold coffee, not wanting it, not wanting anything except to get up and bolt for cover. A slice of toast was left on the plate, cut in two pieces. There were two halves of her, too. That was the trouble. One half wanted freedom, a small taste of which had once been hers. She had never danced on tables, but she had heard the chimes at midnight with Master Shallow before he turned into a rotten dipso. It was the other half, the slow, cautious part giving a dull comfort never far from despair, that held her back. Where had it come from? Of what bitter lees in her man-handled spirit was it composed? Was it the insecurity of her childhood that condemned her? Her abandoned religion, which had filled her with suspicion and dread as a schoolgirl? Fear? Cowardice? Or some source outside all these? A heavy wheel was dragging her downhill, slowly, remorselessly. Was she bound to it forever? "Mine own tears do scald like molten lead," she remembered. That damned play wasn't helping. She searched in her bag for a tissue, found one, dropped it, bent over to pick it up off the floor, and rose to find a beak not six inches from her face.

Oh Jesus, she thought, spare me. "Some good I mean to do despite of mine own nature," said Miss Farmer as, expecting nothing but a cheery welcome, she barged into the booth. "Edmund, of course, act five, after he's had the biscuit. Have I got an idea about that! Mind if I join you? Freezing out, isn't it? So this is where you sneak off, to meet lover boy no doubt. You rascal! I thought I'd have Italian today. Haven't tried this place before. Heard it was a bit grubby. Is the food good? Have you ordered?" A babble about food, her classes, and the weather came forth in a torrent as she settled her mighty torso, took off her muddy boots, rolled up the sleeves of her bulky-knit sweater, and surveyed the scene around her. The three lasagna eaters looked at her. Though tormented with dyspepsia, one managed a smile. Miss Farmer smiled back at him. Correction: leered at all three. They were close to her, and they were men. It was enough to make an occasion. "I know your first name, of course," she said to Jane. "But I don't think I've ever told you mine. It's Faith." Having made this disclosure, she perused the menu with various "oohs" and "ahs," edging closer to Jane all the time, occasionally winking at the drinkers, giggling. Then she ordered spaghetti bolognese "with lots of Parmesan cheese and French bread." Jane decided not to order lunch after all.

"I got my idea yesterday," said Miss Farmer. "You'll be interested in this." The story was of something she'd been asked to do for a special projects committee of the Community Service Council. The Council had decided to extend the weekday service provided to the elderly and disabled by Meals-On-Wheels to the weekend. "You can imagine," she said, "the difficulties of doing such a thing—the negotiations between the organizations, the memos, board meetings, worries about territorial rights, and so on. It took a month for the council to get permission, another two weeks to work out how exactly to deliver the meals. At last it was all ready. Enter Faith."

As a favour to one of the volunteers, she was asked to do something out of the ordinary for a man on Brine Street in the downtown, a known drinker but old and virtually helpless. She was to make him a turkey dinner, because yesterday was his birthday and the word was going around that he mightn't live long. He didn't want a meal brought to him; he wanted one cooked for him, in his home. "Crooked old bugger," Miss Farmer said, laughing. "Still making outrageous demands, still thinking he was important, and nobody giving a hoot for him really, except for one of the volunteers at the council who had him on a list. That's far down the totem pole, Janey."

Anyway, on Saturday she drove to the volunteer's home in a borrowed car —"you may have noticed, I don't have one myself"— got the money for the groceries, and bought them at the Co-op to keep expenses down. "An extra piece of driving for me, time lost, but what the heck." Down she went yesterday to the old fellow's house with a turkey leg, potatoes, frozen peas, a quarter pound of carrots, and tins of gravy and cranberry sauce. "Had to have cranberry, special order. The sheer gall!" She fought her way in through beer bottles and garbage. The stove was in the kitchen in the basement, the old man was in his bed on the third floor. "No talk of trying to get up, my dear. He didn't much like waiting for his dinner, either." The stove didn't work; she found a fuse and made it work. There was no casserole dish to bake the turkey in; she borrowed one from a neighbour. The oven was filthy; she cleaned it. No dishes were clean; so she washed them. "All he used was Lifebuoy soap, honest. A first for me, Lifebuoy on dishes." No can opener could be located for the gravy and cranberry; more borrowing. "Two and a half hours it took me to get that dinner ready. Up the stairs I marched with it. The house was so cold the grease on the plate turned white before I got to the bedroom, so I went down, heated it all again, put it in the casserole with the cover on, and brought it up once more. Hot this time, by golly. Think I was sick of this job by now? You bet."

The old man had turned in to the wall when she finally brought him his dinner. "I propped him up with pillows, wiped his face and hands with a warm facecloth. He took one mouthful of turkey, said he didn't like it, and wouldn't eat another bite."

She then washed the dishes, left the turkey and vegetables for him in the fridge, and returned the utensils she had borrowed. The old cuss only grunted when she went in to say good-bye. Home she went to mark twenty-five essays and prepare the last scenes of *Lear* for today's class.

"Then it hit me. You know, what Edmund says before he dies? The good he wants to do but can't do? I got it, says I. Evil just happens; just let go, hang around, be in the right place, it'll happen. But the good thing takes—well, what does it take?" She threw up her hands. "Look at the turkey dinner. All the planning, effort. And still nothing came of it. That's the worst. What did I accomplish? Nothing at all, love, nothing at all."

As she was telling this, spaghetti, bread, and Parmesan cheese were disappearing, and towards the end, Jane, who was starting to feel hungry, begged a little off her plate. After the bill was paid, Miss Farmer looked at the men again and chuckled at what was happening. It had become quite a spectacle. The wine expert had spilled some of the lasagna—correction, all the lasagna left on his plate—into his lap, and was calling for more booze. "Brandy and soda, my good fellow," he said to the waiter. "Fetch me brandy and soda, the drink of Sir Winston."

All the diners were now laughing and shaking their heads as they left the restaurant. Jane smiled, too, as she hooked her arm into Miss Farmer's and they headed for the car, hurrying to be sure to be in time for the one o'clock bell. Mr. Shannahan was always out in the corridor to see if any of the teachers were late, and it was important to be prompt to give an example to the students. But when she got in the car, Jane decided to slow down. She'd get there without rushing. There was time, lots of time. And as for her lessons, they were so well prepared that it was just a matter of opening her notebook and she was ready.

Lights out

Come over. Closer. Put your pillow next to mine. That's better.

You very sleepy? Neck still hurting? Cranky? I can't seem to doze off. You don't mind if I talk a bit, do you? Can I ask you something? You know our *annus mirabilis?* How do you feel, now that it's over? Happier than you were? Contented, at least? Accept your decision?

All right, say nothing. I know it's more than one question. "You say you've got a question, then you ask me seven." I can hear you now. No, don't turn over. I can't talk to you that way. I can't confide in a back. A back is not an intimate object, not to me, anyway. Did the other one like your back, as well as the useful parts?

Sorry, that was a slip.

So, turn over. Just don't drop off on me, that's all. I've been thinking. About how we raised the girls and the arguments we had over them. We had some doozers, didn't we? If we only had one per girl per year, that'd be twenty for each one, for a total of sixty. And we had a lot more than one a year, right? What's the matter, my math wrong? Oh, don't rumble at me. Soften up a little. I didn't mean to mention her. She just flashed through my mind.

Remember how it was with the girls? Me wanting rules for everything, beds made, toys picked up, school uniform on, certain hours off the phone—small things, but to me they counted. You'd let them go out in sneakers and shorts in a snowstorm. Anything for a bit of peace. Your motto.

It's a wonder they turned out as well as they did, with all the bickering they heard between us. Children take advantage of inconsistency. I told you they would, didn't I?

Don't be an old grouch. Answer me.

You were the hero, of course. Good old Dad, he'll let you do anything. Real sport, Dad is. St. Francis Flynn, late of the outharbours, local notable, in *Who's Who*, for God's sake. A marvel! Did I get mad a few hundred times? Little wonder.

You asleep? Move an arm. Ok.

Then there was the house. How much I wanted to keep it clean and tidy, everything in its place. I got that from mother. I know, I know, you didn't marry mother, you married me. Don't glare. I can feel you glaring.

You'd come barging in after work looking for a place to whack down your briefcase, and I'd have daffs on the table, maybe, or nice cloths, and wouldn't want your old briefcase put down there or anywhere, remember? And you'd say something like, "I was over at Tom Ghaney's today for lunch. He's got a special table in the hall for his briefcase." It didn't occur to me to ask why you went to a nuclear physicist's for lunch instead of coming home. Stupid of me not to ask. Or you might say, "Donna, I paid Jesus knows how much for this house and every stick of furniture in it. Can I have a place to lay down my briefcase?" I'd find you a spot, after a while. There was no need to do what you did to the black case a few years ago, the one I gave you. That was sinful, that was. I could skin you alive sometimes.

Don't get so flaming mad over little things. How many times have I told you that? And, by the way, what was that about you paying for everything? Is this a partnership or isn't it? Well?

Now don't fall off on me. Don't, ok? This is leading to something. I'm just doing it in my usual "goddamned roundabout way," to quote you. That's a very nice thing to be saying, by the way. Nature's gentleman, you are. But stick with me, that's all I'm asking. I did a lot of thinking today. My head's been spinning.

And the rackets over the lawn. You slacking off on Saturday or Sunday, watching the Blue Jays, me wanting the front mowed, the back raked, flowers planted, the shed painted. I want to bring that in, too. It's a seamless garment I'm weaving. You'll see.

What's the matter? Pillow too soft? I must get you one of those beauty-rest pillows. They have them at a shop over by Sobey's for a hundred and thirty-five dollars. I know it's only October, but it'll be one of your Christmas presents. I got lots for you already. You bought anything yet? I know you're not a believer, but if it'll make you feel any better the Jehovah's Witnesses say it's a pagan festival. Myself, I kind of believe in it. Sometimes.

And the parties. Me wanting to go out and meet some people, you with your head in the books preparing lectures on Melville or some transcendentalist. A cracker jack at a party, you were. I'd look around half an hour after we got somewhere, and you'd be in a corner by the bookcase, looking at titles, maybe even reading. Who'd believe it, reading *Billy Budd* at a party? I'd go over and haul you off to talk to somebody. "Be sociable, for God's sake," I'd say.

You'd try, sometimes. If the music wasn't too loud. I can see you now, standing around in people's rec rooms, music blaring, a glass of coke in your hand, trying to get with it. "I had a great evening," you'd say after, "talked to one kid and barked at two dogs." Why you had to be so, so *awkward*, was beyond me. Everyone else would be in the mood, or in the sauce, or into something. But you'd be out of it, off in your head somewhere.

Then on the four or five occasions out of the—oh, I don't know, fifty? —when you did manage to get a bit social, it didn't always turn out the way I'd hoped. I'll never forget the night at Scott Davis's place, when the music was turned down at last and the dancing stopped, and we could all hear you and Joan Ghaney in the kitchen arguing. I went out to have a look. She wasn't fat then. Not that she was ever thin, but she wasn't plump. You get the point. You probably lifted her a few times. Sorry. I remember she had her glasses off and was really giving it to you. Holding her own, no question. "The important thing is to have something to give to people, not to be looking up your navel all the time," she was saying, "That's my philosophy."

"Here's a sharp knife," says you, opening a drawer and taking out one that looked like it could cut through an iron pot. "Give it to young Jim here. He's people. See what he'll do with a piece of your philosophy." And poor, retarded Jimmy Davis looking on, wondering what the racket was about, with the hand out for the knife he was hoping to use to cut off the cat's tail, maybe. It was some scene, I can tell you. You looked like you were in the juice. I knew you weren't, of course, and should have spotted trouble. If it wasn't whiskey or gin, it had to be something else that lit your wick.

You thought you had her. I could see your look. But she came back, and I thought, good for you Joan, wish I'd stood up to him more. I was just about beaten by then, see. She wasn't. "Don't try your mind games on me, Frank," she said. "You're just trying to bury me in that grave you're in. You're a cynic, something's coarsened you. Go to hell." That stung you. You put that knife away damn fast.

We had it out later, remember? In the car? A slam-banger, that one. Donna's last stand. Me defending Joan! I can't believe it now. But I did. Poor foolish me. What she said about being buried made sense. I always felt you thought women were simple. That's been part of the trouble. It's what drove me to feminism. Not that I was ever much of a feminist, but you know what I mean. Leaning that way. I was afraid of getting buried alive by you—you and your books. I had to find a way to breathe. That's why I put so much into the kids and house. My territory, sort of. No Trespassing sign on it.

Not that you were the only one to get in trouble at parties. Remember that night at Searle's, when we were asked to leave their house? You probably forget. I said something—it was a very innocent remark, honest—to one of their guests, some hysterical peroxide blonde half-crazed with booze and tranquilizers and self-importance. Into interior decorating now, I hear. She may be able to tell an apple from an orange. That's what she knows about colours. Anyway, there was a racket. Only one woman stood up for me. Can't think of her name. It'll come to me. Brace, maybe, something like that. Never saw her again. But the blonde bitch asked the host to kick us out, and good old Bill, full of character, as usual, went along with her. She was part of his gang. We weren't. He may have had something going with her on the side, for all I know. I've learned a few things since that night.

I looked over my shoulder, hoping you were there to help me. I needed help from you that night, pal. Sure, I'd stepped out of line a little—a minor gaffe, nothing serious. But the effects! It wasn't just the embarrassment of the moment. It was the way it made me feel about myself, as if I were somebody who could be discarded without fear or loss, an insect to be trod on. You know what I mean? I had an idea of what I was, what we were. Bill squat it.

So I looked around for you to take my part. That's what husbands are for, don't you know that yet? Don't you know anything? Transcendentalism! I could strangle you sometimes. Couldn't find you. When I put my coat on and went to look for you, there you were on the veranda, talking to Joan again. In the moonlight! I should've clawed her eyes out. No arguments this time, only sweet looks. The philosophers had made up. I think she'd even persuaded you to have a glass of wine, and I can only guess what she must have offered to make you do that. The thought didn't even cross my mind that you were up to something with her. If it did, I can't recall it. Maybe I was so anxious to get out of the Searles' yuppie slum that I didn't notice.

Was Peace her name? You know, the woman who helped me? That's a surname. Bet you didn't even know that.

Looking back now, I realize that all the signs were lit up ages ago, but stupid me, I didn't know until the *mirabilis* that something was desperately wrong. A squalid affair, after all those years! You cruise along, wham! you get it between the eyes. How could you even think of it, after so long? Louse.

And we've had some good times, haven't we? In the early years? That's undeniable. Agree? In fact, I can picture the first time you caught my eye. It was in the advanced Shakespeare class, when old Hunter asked what Cordelia did wrong in Act I of *Lear*. The way he asked the question, we all assumed she *had* done something wrong, so we attacked her judgment, prudence, foresight, the usual things. You were just another bayman sitting in the back, to me, then. But when Hunter got to you, you said one word, "Nothing."

"What's that, young man?" said Hunter.

"Nothing," says you. "She did nothing wrong."

And then you went on to say that it was Lear who committed the wrong. Cordelia had offered him half her love, you said, and that was a lot. "How many people get offered any?" I think I can give you back the very words you used that day, so long ago. "When love comes knocking, you're a fool not to open the door." Well, we all turned around to see who this upstart was, and I saw the boy I would chase for the next three years. I knocked a hundred times a week for you, wise guy, that's a thousand and forty knocks. Minimum. The hinges should be worn off that door by now.

Don't nod off. I'm coming to the hard part. I can hear your breath getting heavy.

That brings me to last year, the night you told me. I don't think you remember all the details. But I do, every one. You had been pushed around too long, you said. You wanted freedom. No more boring parties, stupid plays, and concerts. No more being dragged off to places you hated. Out of the house you were marching.

This time I wasn't so dumb as not to know there had to be another woman, and I had a pretty good idea of the sparkling creature's name. As you were making your long speech, you know what I was thinking? Two things. Number one, I thought I could say the very same things to you that you were saying to me. In spades. Freedom! Sixties rubbish. Who is it that hasn't had the clamps put on at our age? Tell me that. Clamps of time, children. Responsibility. Put that among your big words, genius. The second thing, and I mean this, I'm not trying to be a stinker. It's going to hurt, but you have to pay attention. For the first time in my life, as I listened to you I thought you looked old. Something had happened to your face, or else what you said to me made me look at it in a new way. It wasn't coarsened, exactly. Fat Joanie wasn't altogether right. It looked bilious, craven. It had sagged. I noticed your belly too, as you lugged the green garbage bags full of clothes out to the car, puffing and blowing. It, well, it protruded, Frank. A little. But there it was, flab. Not a nice thought, flab. First time I'd noticed that, too.

I wasn't surprised—I have to tell you the truth—when you phoned up two hours later and said the experiment was over. That was the word you used, experiment. Academic to the end. Me in the test tube, I guess, fatso the Bunsen burner, you the gas. Listen, do me a favour, will you? If I die before you, don't fucking experiment with my carcass, ok? Just put me six feet under. Ok, Frank?

"I'd like to come back, old thing," you said. Very romantic. No sign of Cordelia in that, Frank. And so you did. You never said why you came back. I haven't been told to this day who called it off. Don't want to tell me now, do you? I know, anyway.

Now I guess I should say what I've been leading up to for the past half hour. It's not too late to talk of forgiveness. Forgiveness isn't just for the young, as you think. There's no age limit on it, you don't transcend it. You don't know everything. I'm still a believer, in a way. I'll get around to it one of these days.

But here's what's on my mind. You know what I used to say about the girls and the house and the lawn, my neatness, my feeling that I had to stand up to you, my feminism, half-hearted as it was— all the things you thought of as obstacles and miseries? Guess what? I'm over all that now. It's all behind me. I didn't do it for you, it just happened. Maybe it's biological or something.

You know what I thought today? This is something to build on. Eyes front. My new motto.

We can start again, sort of. I'll take a small life, if that's what it's got to be. The other thing might even come back. I'm hopeful. We can still go places.

Can't we, old dog? Tell me we can.

Asleep? Headache?
Move a leg, damn it!
I got it! It was Grace, it was Grace!
Was that it? Oh, tell me, was it?

Surrender

It will take a few months, he thought. The thing was to get through the hard part without damage. Time would do the rest. Poets might write of undying love, but he was forty and had seen the years take their toll of memory and desire. Toughen it out, he said to himself. It will pass. Hold the fort.

The first week went by smoothly. When he came to look, he realized how little she had given him. A few knickknacks, a little bottle, a book; that was it. The bottle, though, was special. She had brought that back to him from a holiday in the Caymans with her stupid, rich husband. It had a ship in it and the colour of the sails was hazel, the same as her eyes. "It will remind you of me," she said. "Keep it always." It was the kind of thing she said, straight out of books and movies.

It drove him crazy. When he questioned her excess, she said again, "Always. Keep it, and you'll never leave me, nor I you."

So much for words. He found a safe harbour for the bottle and other objects, moved the furniture around in his office, bought himself bright ties, striped shirts, and tight pants—the kind she hated—and marched forward into the world. She had made him too solitary. He needed to mix with people, talk it up. He had been a great talker before he met her, and could be so again. He'd show her. He joined a darts' league and a bridge club, went to church for the first time in months—she loathed religion—and got mixed up in politics again. Finding himself reviving, he even ventured to ask one of her friends how she was doing. "Forget it," he was told. "She's satisfied now. It's as if she has a new life. Don't butt in." One evening as he sat talking to a couple of graduate students in a tavern, he got a glimpse of himself in the mirror over the bar, making some point or other about society, the way he used to years before. Shortly after he got up and went home.

He caught himself sometimes speaking aloud to her, rehearsing his usual arguments. "No, it's not good enough, this catting around. Look, think of it this way. I'm a door that's swinging open. There's a better life for you through me. The door might shut. Grab the chance." He had used up his store of analogies on her. One day he was mouthing the tightrope argument—"I'm on a tightrope, I've fallen, I'm hanging on, come out and haul me up!"—and a surly-looking man stopped him by the supermarket; in fact, grabbed him by the shoulder. "I've been listening to you, pal," he said, "Is there a circus in town?"

The first month ended with his spirits intact, though he felt it was best to stay away from the shops she frequented and avoid the routes she took to work. At first he found roundabout ways to drive, but then he thought that just being in a car was dangerous because you had to keep looking up and down streets for traffic and pedestrians. So before long he started to walk to work in order to be able to use back alleys and paths through the parks. It was time for him to think of the great outdoors anyway and to take up a number of new interests. That was what the doctor had advised. It made sense. She had kept him indoors too much. The walking pleased him because he felt it was good for his lungs and heart muscles. Thinking it wise to make changes in other areas of his life, he switched supermarkets, banks, churches, dry cleaners, hairdressers, drugstores, and parking lots. There weren't many things left to change. It was best not to take chances.

In his second month he decided to stay away at night from movies that might have attracted her—she liked sentimental American films, westerns, anything Swedish and sexy—and to dig into his reading, where he had a lot of catching up to do. His hobby was history, with the North American frontier being a special interest. A number of titles had been piling up from his book club in the past year, among them a history of Louisbourg, a novel about pioneer days in Alberta, a biography of William Lyon Mackenzie, and collections of early American poetry. He put the verse to one side and burrowed into Louisbourg. It took a long time to read the book, which pleased him. He thought he would look for similar studies of Lower Fort Garry and Fort Chimo. Further south, Ticonderoga beckoned and The Alamo. And the Hudson's Bay Company had just been written up. A month's reading, at least, awaited him there. When he got through that, he might tackle the *Dictionary of Canadian Biography*. So his evenings would be looked after for some months, maybe years. In these circumstances, the bridge club wasn't practical, so he pulled out. With the extra reading, he was putting on *Rigoletto* or *Aida* and falling asleep early. So much the better.

By the end of his third month without her, he had taken a number of extra steps that could only be of benefit. While walking, he would occasionally catch glimpses of someone who looked a little like her. There might be a certain toss of the head, turn of the chin, clumsy way of walking, flash of white teeth, impatient gesture with the hands, or none of these but some indescribable grace that called her to mind when he was deep in thought about the voyageurs battling their way across the prairie or Pierre Le Moyne D'Iberville ravaging the English shore in Newfoundland. He always looked away fast when he saw such things, but by then the harm had been done. To counter this, he decided to look straight ahead and down as he walked to his office, and to glance in no cars whatsoever. There was no telling what you might catch sight of there. People riding along in cars didn't seem to think the world could look in on them. The strategy of not looking helped, though he was forced to move his eyes up sometimes, at intersections for instance, and there was then the possibility of coming to grief.

He continued to work on this, but it wasn't the only problem he had. Defend one corner, another lay exposed. When he was in the supermarket, or at parties, staff meetings, or other common gatherings, he would hear echoes in somebody's voice that reminded him of her. It might be a tinkle of laughter, squeal of joy, whisper, chuckle, or grammatical peculiarity. She had her own way of saying certain words and phrases. "Tell me that again," she might say to him after he had told her some story about Poundmaker or Benedict Arnold, "tell me that again, will ya"; and it was the way she said the "will ya" that knocked him over. A gentle, innocent way. He couldn't bear to hear anybody else say it. But people did use the phrase. In fact, they used it more and more as time passed. Even educated people used it, damn them.

He came up with the idea of wearing earplugs, but this would call attention to him. He bought a pair of plugs anyway, just in case he was ever in a spot where he couldn't avoid listening to someone who sounded a bit like her or who said "will ya": in an airplane, say, or at a dinner party. He actually stuck a plug in once at a darts tournament, explaining to his captain that the ear in question was sore. To discover the right defence in this area was not easy. What he found himself doing was staying away from crowds, and reconnoitring a room carefully for sights and sounds—and in time even smells, because she had her own odour too—before going in and settling down to mix with people. A few times he thought it best to beat a quick retreat, hoping that this wouldn't be commented on. His invitations to dinner declined in number.

Six months passed without her. He noticed that he was hearing awkward things in conversations. Now that the whisperings about him and her had stopped, people would carelessly let slip that she had been seen with so-and-so at a movie, that she had joined a cult devoted to the pursuit of world peace through art—which greatly amused him because he had taught her what little she knew about art and literature—or that she was going off to the Virgin Islands on holiday with such-and-such a one. Perhaps someone would say he had seen her working out at a health club or jogging. She had always stayed in shape and watched her health, eating carrot cake and nuts, which she maddeningly claimed gave her eyes their colour. These casual mentions of her name were worse than the direct questions put to him when they first broke up, and presented another problem. He solved it by keeping more and more to himself. He stayed out of the cafeteria where he had been going for years to chat with co-workers, and yielded up his place on committees. He even dropped the dart league. For a while a few people phoned up to ask how he was doing. Then that stopped, and apart from routine contacts at his job, he found himself safe from risky conversations.

Of course, his buddies at work mentioned her now and then. There was that to consider. Sometimes he felt like not talking at all, to anyone. He began phoning in sick a few times a month just to have a perfectly safe day. Rather than go to the supermarket, on occasion he phoned out for fried chicken, pizza, or other supplies. Running into friends after church, he decided, might create trouble. He stopped going.

After a year he just about had all his problems licked. Only one remained, but it was a big one. Her face! He couldn't get her face out of his mind. As he looked down during his walks, it wasn't the pavement he was seeing now but her face. When he stared at the sea on his long tramps over Signal Hill, he could see it. The sky had it; the stars at night. He woke up with it on his mind. This perplexed him, as he had been sure that in a few months the memory of the way her hair curled around her ears, the way she smiled, grimaced, lifted her eyebrows, would vanish. Of course he expected the broad outline to stay with him, but not the details. These, the treacherous heart kept smuggling in, despite all he could muster in barricades and diversions. More steps were called for.

Late on Saturday afternoons, when most of those who knew him had gone to the country, he ventured out and borrowed books on painting from the public library. He then sat for hours in his apartment poring over the faces of beautiful women in Gainsborough, Rubens, Vermeer, da Vinci, Goya, memorizing the size of their ears, the shape of their lips, studying their noses and cheekbones, relishing their eyes. The way to drive her out was to let classic beauty in, he figured. When this produced only small gains, he turned to ugly and plain women: Hogarth's whores, Bruegel's peasants, the Medusa, Sin and Death, lepers. These absorbed him more. Committed to memory, they could be summoned up to be his companions in the long nights. Velasquez's tearstained, pudgy Martha was his favourite. He took time off work to follow this new tack and spent hours contemplating the whores and Martha, his chosen company.

One morning he woke up and found himself dreaming of Martha. She was weeping and he was trying to console her, but couldn't find the right words. His mouth and throat were dry; and there was really nothing to say. He reached out and, not finding her, got off his couch and managed to call her name. No answer. Strange! He called again. Where had she gone? He called a third time, a fourth, feeling his voice strengthen. Again and again he called. Soon there was a knocking at his door and he went to it, knowing she had come back to him. He could not feign indifference as he drew back the heavy bolts and turned the knob to let her in.

The other lion

Jimmy Byrne's eleventh year was spoiled, and it was mostly because of Pad and Dan Oliver from Gull Island, a place about a mile down the shore from his home in Long Beach. If you just heard the name somewhere you'd think it really was an island, but it wasn't. It was only another outport. Jimmy's family owned hay meadows there near Gull Island Brook, and in August he liked going down to help rake up the hay and ride back in the hay crate on top of the last load. He would lie back in the hay, watch the clouds making shapes in the sky, and listen to the horse's tackling squeak and rattle. It was fun not to look at the houses on the highroad, and try to guess how far you'd come on the way home. The smell of the horse and the hay was good, too.

One day when he was still nine, the crate went up with a full load and he was left behind to prong and rake more hay into little pooks to make it easy to pick up. "Watch you don't stab yourself with that prong," his father said. As soon as the crate left, Pad and Dan caught him lying down getting a drink from the brook and ducked him. He had been ducked before, but only when he was in deep swimming holes or in Gull Island Pond, where many of the boys congregated on hot afternoons in summer. He was only a middling swimmer, but good enough to stay out of trouble. This time they held his head down so long that he got frightened and had to breathe in. He splashed and kicked, to no avail. They wouldn't let him up. His face rubbed against the rocks so that mud was stirred up and he couldn't see anything. When he was just about gone and had stopped kicking, they hauled him back and ran away fast because they thought he would throw rocks at them. But he couldn't even get up. His breath wouldn't come, and he vomited. He had to stay down to keep his head from spinning, while they sat on a fence and just about killed themselves laughing. When the crate came back, he didn't tell his father about the ducking or try to explain why he was cross.

Jimmy got over this fast, but remembered it when he went back in the fall to look at his favourite picture at school. This was in a book the new teacher for some reason kept in a closet. It was called "The Deluge." In it a lot of half-naked people were climbing up a steep rock that was surrounded by bubbling white surf. There were some naked ones as well, but you couldn't really see anything. Some of the climbers held onto little girls as they tried to get out of the water, or clung to the branches and stump of a dead tree that had washed up. Some were lying on their backs, either dead or resting. It was hard to tell which. There was a lion in the tree, too. A couple of women were swimming towards the rock, but one man had let go and his head was down in the white water. You could tell he was a goner.

The closet had no light bulb, and he didn't much like being in a place that would be totally dark if somebody closed the door. In fact, Pad had slammed it shut one day at recess and it took Jimmy a good while to get out. That was scary. But he got a secret feeling of excitement from looking at the picture, especially at the lion. It was crouching on a limb of the tree, trying not to fall off, not hurting anyone. It looked tired and scared, just like the people. It was funny there was only one. Maybe there was another lion out in back of the rock, he thought. There had to be lots of things happening on the other side of the rock too, even though you couldn't see them.

When it was raining, most of the pupils would go and get a Hardy Boys book or one of the *Books of Knowledge* at recess time. The *Books of Knowledge* were new in the school. Dan always got down the *National Geographic*, and Jimmy, before joining him for a peek at the African women, would sneak off to the closet to look at the lion. He didn't need the new teacher to tell him how much there was to know about the world beyond Newfoundland. He had always wanted to learn about things. He knew there were mysteries, deep waters he couldn't see into. A looker, his mother called him. "Poking your nose in again," she'd say when he tried to see what she was doing in the pantry or parlour. He was there looking on when his father stuck the pig and drained the blood into buckets to make black puddings, and when he cut the throats of the lambs. Seeing the guts of fish being taken out didn't bother him at all. In fact, he could gut fish himself. He was in the stable one year looking when the cow calved. He wanted to see what the priest was up to when he bent over the wine and water on the altar and whispered. Most people put their heads down when this was happening. He kept his up.

At school, he mixed with the Gull Islanders, who were said to be a hard bunch. Pad and Dan were his friends, despite what they did to him in the brook. He was ten now and didn't hold grudges. Although they were much older than him, Dan by two years, Pad by three, he was only a grade behind them. He always walked home with the Gull Island crowd. Corpus Christi school was at the upper end of Long Beach, and his house was near the lower end, down a lane from the main road. Getting down the lane was not easy. The trick was to watch your chance and run like crazy before the Gull Islanders noticed you were gone. As soon as they saw Jimmy or one of his brothers running, they made for the side of the road to pick up rocks, which would whiz by. Jimmy wasn't fast, but he was tricky and had been hit only once in many dashes down the lane.

One day he stayed behind with Pad and Dan and some other boys after school to listen to what the teacher had to say about making a hockey rink on Long Beach Pond, a long shallow gully in back of the priest's grove. It was so shallow that you couldn't even swim in it in summer. The teacher was organizing sports to keep the boys out of mischief. Pad and Dan, unlike most Gull Islanders, had turned out to be good skaters. Going down the road afterwards, Jimmy made his usual fast break for the house and he could hear Pad say, "Quick, get the rocks and let him have it!" He was at the bottom of the lane when he realized not a rock had been thrown. "They're good boys," his father said later when Jimmy was helping him saw firewood. His father's mother had been born and raised in Gull Island, which was why they had meadows down by the brook.

Pad and Dan were among the first of Jimmy's friends to smoke. He was walking by the priest's grove on his way in to work on the hockey rink, and saw the two of them, with Marie Kelloway from the school and a girl he didn't recognize, sitting under a tree smoking. He might have seen the girl once before, when the Western Bay hockey team came down and beat Corpus Christi 23-1. The teacher now had a North Shore Hockey League going. Dan waved the cigarette pack at him. "Come on in, Jim, and have a Camel," he said.

"And if you don't want a Camel, you can get a hump," said the girl he didn't know.

"Get a what?" Jimmy asked.

"Come in, I got a bush here I want to show you," she said.

Pad, Dan, and Marie all laughed at that. Although he wanted to see what they were doing in the grove, Jimmy went about his business. Not that he had much to do that day. There was a bit of wood to split when he got home, that was all. He thought he might try a cigarette later when Pad and Dan were by themselves. It seemed like a lot of fun.

They had picked up the smoking habit from their brothers, Dan told him. One of their brothers, Phil, worked at Stephenville on the American base, and another, Jim, in the mines on Bell Island. Jim was known all around Bell Island as a quiet fellow you didn't meddle with. A foreman named Lynch from Carbonear picked on him for about a month when Jim first went to work in the mines, calling him a North Shore pork-eater and a bay noddy. When he had enough of this he struck Lynch, knocked him flat with one punch, and broke his jaw in four places. Lynch was sucking on a straw for six weeks. "Served him right," Jimmy's father said. "Finest kind of a man, Jim Oliver." Pad and Dan would go away as soon as they finished school. Having long been a skeptic about schools and colleges, their father now believed in the value of education, and insisted that both boys finish their grade eleven before they got out of Gull Island. Mr. Oliver had been coming back in his skiff from Bay de Verde one stormy evening ten years before, and realized the only thing keeping him and Phil from their doom was the spark in an old 6-Atlantic engine. "That was it, that minute," he told Jimmy's father. "No more fishing for me." Since then, not one of his sons had put a foot in a boat to go fishing.

The last winter of Jimmy's boyhood was a cold one, and the hockey rink was in constant use. After the beating by

Western Bay, Corpus Christi played Upper Island Cove and lost 16-1. "That's progress," the teacher said. Indeed, the team was improving and in early January lost to Western Bay by one goal. Jimmy was the goaltender sometimes, but he was too slow to be a winger like Dan. Since he was good at words, the teacher let him put a name on the team. He chose "Lions." He was getting interested in a play the teacher was putting on, in which he had to do the monkey dance. There was also science to wonder about, the school having bought some lab equipment for the senior grades. Jimmy could only look at the magnets and test tubes; he would have to wait until next year to get his hands on them. The older boys seemed to have a great time with the iron filings and litmus paper.

So caught up was he with school and other things that, as the weeks passed, he almost forgot to go to the closet. Dan let him try a cigarette, which made him sick, so he went no further with that. An experiment with malt beer brought a similar result. He found out what Marie and the girl he didn't know had been trying to get Pad and Dan to do under the tree, and wanted to look into that, too. The girl had, in fact, come up to him after a game and offered to help him take his goalie pads off as he was sitting on the ice. Her hair was tied behind her head and she had nice clothes on. Up-the-shore clothes. He said "No, thanks" to her offer, but kept his eye on her as she moved off the pond with the Western Bay crowd. She looked back at him twice. Maybe he could have a lot of fun with her.

The winter deepened and interest in hockey fell off. Soon it would be "the long and hungry month of March" when the men headed to St. John's for the seal hunt. His father got his gear ready for the kill. His berth was with Captain Wes Kean on the *Blue Peter* again, although the ship had been stuck for sixty-four days in the ice last year. But the weather had turned warm and this spring might be better. "Mind that axe when I'm gone," he told Jimmy, who was to be in charge of firewood, "I just got it sharpened." Jimmy's mother grumbled. She was left home with five youngsters, and look who her man was sailing with. "Some captain," she said.

One day after school was over and he was out by the woodpile making splits for the next morning's fire, Jimmy looked up on the ridge behind Long Beach and saw dozens of people rushing towards Gull Island Pond. He ran in to see what was happening, taking a short cut through a grove, over snow that was dirty and soft because of the thaw. As he got to the top of the ridge, he could see a bunch of men and women by the side of the pond. A dory was out in the water where the ice had been broken in.

"Four men went through the ice," someone said, passing him. "But they got 'em out."

"Who?" Jimmy called. There was no answer.

Why would four men be out on Gull Island Pond at this time of year? It was too late for horses and slides to be going inland for wood. It made no sense. He came near the side of the pond and, not wanting to push through the crowd right away, got on a rock to look over the heads of the men and women. "It's Pad and Dan, two of 'em," a voice whispered.

"Dan went through first, and Pad went in after him," said another.

"Dan grabbed the edge of the ice, but it kept breaking and the current took him under," said a third. "There's a bad current in the pond, and that's the deepest part."

"No, that's not as deep as up by the brook," someone said. "It's ten fathom up there."

Now there was a hubbub of voices, with some saying that Pad had managed to get his skates off before going in the water for Dan, and others denying this. Most agreed that Dan had shouted to his brother not to come in, although one woman said the opposite, that Dan had begged him for help. But there was no denying that Pad had gone in and held onto Dan for a while before letting him go. Then he went under himself. Nobody could get near them because the ice was too soft. The only safe way to get them was to work from the dory, which had to be dragged up from the foot of the pond. They hadn't been hauled out of the water for ten, maybe fifteen minutes.

Stretching hard, Jimmy saw Pad and Dan, their skates off, being rolled over barrels to get the water out of their lungs. They were then laid on blankets on their backs and worked on. He kept his distance and watched for a long while from his rock. The doctor turned up and said "Open their chests." He put his instrument on each of them and pushed hard, listening; went back to Dan, pushed harder, listened.

"It's too late. They're gone," he said. "Take 'em out."

Jimmy walked forward among the sobbing, shrieking women to look at his friends' almost purple faces. Water and snot were dribbling out of Pad's nose. Dan's mouth and cheek were cut. There was no mistaking what they were; they weren't resting. Staying to the end, he watched the men take the bodies off the rocks and lug them along the side of the pond in the blankets. He looked then at the black, cold, deep water and, knowing as much as he would ever want to know about the world he couldn't see, turned his back and walked away.

"These things happen in threes," he heard someone say as he left the pond. Had he left the axe near the chopping block where his little sisters might find it? He made a fast break for home.

The coat

In his young days, Abe Foley of Northern Bay was a master fisherman, but by the age of forty he saw that the days of cod traps, trawls, and hand-lines were finished on the shore. He told his three sons to find other jobs, which they did, one becoming a vet, one a merchant, and the youngest, John, a university teacher in a discipline as remote from the backbreaking and dangerous business of fishing as it was possible to get—fine arts. "John is in the arts line," Abe would say when somebody asked him what his sons were doing; or, perhaps, "John gets paid for what he knows, not for what he does." Then he'd add: "Not that he does nothing, mind." At times all this would provoke a laugh or two, but Abe well knew what an advantage it was to have regular money coming in, whatever the source. "I wish I'd gone into arts myself when I was a young fellow," he'd say to his neighbours. "Nobody around here could make windjacks as good as mine."

Now if any one of his sons had an aptitude for fishing, that son was John. By his mid-twenties, he would come out from St. John's on the weekends to help his father catch salmon, a fishery still yielding modest returns which the crafty veteran was not willing to abandon. The weekends stretched into weeks, and before long John bought an old house a few miles up the road from his father in a place called Ochre Pit Cove.

It was at the government wharf in Ochre Pit Cove that Abe moored his eighteen-foot boat, which was driven by a twenty-five horsepower outboard motor. Abe was a believer in the Johnson over the Evinrude, though his preference on this point was disputed by some of the men on the wharf, who argued that the Johnson was harder to start and used more gas. One or two of the young fishermen were even switching to Suzukis. "Goes good with the Jap traps," they said. John was known as a good hand with engines. He had just the right touch with the choke. The choke was the key in handling a Johnson, he'd say when outboards came up for discussion. The fishermen would nod when he said this.

Occasionally, when Abe wasn't feeling up to it, John would go out to the nets on his own, and his father would keep an eye on him through the binoculars as he drove the boat carefully along the side of each net, looking for the telltale gleam of silver in the twine below. This steering alongside the net required some skill. If the tide was strong and moving in the same direction as the wind, the twine might billow up under the boat and get tangled in the propeller; if wind and tide were in opposite directions, he had to keep perilously close to the corked headropes in order to see the salmon, if salmon there were, on the other side of the net. Either way, the shear pin on the propeller was in jeopardy. Abe kept extra shear pins and the necessary tools in a bucket in the fore cuddy of the boat. But even such a simple procedure as replacing a shear pin might be risky in the salmon berths, which were normally close to the rocks so that the fish would be netted as they swam around the headlands. When John spotted a salmon, he stopped the engine and tipped it out of the water, then caught hold of the net and pulled towards the fish. That was also tricky, especially in a loppy sea. He was glad the binoculars were sweeping over him every three or four minutes as he worked the nets alone. He felt safe then. In somebody's pocket, he used to say.

With John and Abe taking the lead, the salmon fishery showed signs of expanding. One day they took three nets aboard the boat and steamed to the back of Western Bay Point a couple of miles away to find new berths. These unfamiliar waters were shunned by most fishermen because of strong tides, and handling the nets and six grapelins turned out to be even harder than they had imagined. When they got back to the wharf in the drizzling rain, they decided to drive to Western Bay in the pick-up to see if the nets were afloat and fishing. On the sideroad to the Point, the pick-up got stuck in deep ruts. They walked to the home of a mechanic named Jim Crummey to ask if he would come with one of his big dump trucks to haul them out. Jim looked at them from his doorstep. "Boys, you'm as hard as dogs," he said.

Wet and cold, they got the pick-up out of the mud and returned to Northern Bay. Abe went down into his basement and came up holding an overcoat that had, he thought, once belonged to his grandfather. It could have come from the old sod, that's how old it was. "I can't wear it any more," he said. "The last time I had it on was, oh, six, seven years ago. It's been in mothballs in the storeroom ever since. You take it. No need to bring it back. It'll keep you warm on your way up the shore." And so it did.

John hung the coat in the back porch of his house in Ochre Pit Cove. It wasn't good enough to go in the front hall with his raglan and tweed jacket, and there was no question of taking it to the city. The material in it, though worn, was not threadbare. Two of the brass buttons in front were missing, but the collar was big and John found it was possible to wrap himself so thoroughly in the folds of the coat that the elements could barely get through. Late on a cold night in the spring or fall, when he had to fetch firewood from the barn, he would put it on. Nobody else wore it. It was too long and heavy for his boys, and it wasn't a good fit even on him. His wife Evelyn thought it was dirty and ugly. "You're not going out in that thing, John!" she'd say, if she saw him put it on to go and mail a letter at the post office. "What will people think?" There was indeed nothing stylish about the coat, and yet from a certain angle, in a certain light, it might be thought to have a homespun elegance. This venerable quality could be seen only by John, but, as he explained to Evelyn, he was in the arts and had an eye for such things.

The coat had two side pockets that had been repaired often and were, as a consequence, of different depths. A third one inside the left armpit had been sewn up. Lumps at certain places in the lining suggested that over the decades detritus of various kinds, perhaps a handkerchief, cigarette papers, and even a piece of headgear, had fallen through the holes in the pockets into the gulfs below. Of course, this made the thing heavier, but John wore it so little that it was hardly worth the bother to clean it up and fuss with it.

A few years passed, the salmon fishery declined along the shore, and Abe gave it up altogether to concentrate on planting orange lilies in front of his bungalow and making his soul. But he kept watch over the sea with his binoculars, and left the boat moored near Ochre Pit Cove wharf in case it was needed by his sons for cod-jigging or birding. John's old house, meanwhile, was being changed into a proper country home by the addition of carpets, new window frames, and ranch-style wall panelling. A few paintings and objets d'art were placed in the front room. The kids even put up a sign: "Ocean Manor." When renovations reached the back porch, Evelyn moved the coat to the barn. There it was more liable to have paint dropped on it or to be nibbled by mice. Once John found it in the stable loft stuck up on sticks like a scarecrow, where the kids had placed it to serve some purpose in their games. Another day he found it near the garbage can a half-hour before the collection. Both times he retrieved it and put it back in the corner by the paint cans. He now hardly ever wore it, preferring heavy-knit Irish wool sweaters and light Canadian-made rainwear, but when he hauled loads of kelp or manure for his vegetable garden he put it on, and sometimes, too, when he dug around the septic tank in cold weather. Two more brass buttons fell off, leaving only one, and that dangling by a few threads.

Soon Ocean Manor was refined enough to receive visitors. One of the pleasures John could offer his guests was a day of cod-jigging on the inshore grounds. On a fine day in the summer of his thirty-fifth year, he took his friend Robert Mullaly, who was visiting the province from Toronto, and Robert's sons Liam and Declan, around the bay to go on just such an excursion, leaving his own family in St. John's. A poet and international expert on Celtic literature, Robert had been on the radio calling on Newfoundlanders to get to know the roots of their culture. He had a pocketful of lapel pins, displaying the tri-color of the Irish Republic, that he passed out to all and sundry.

Normally John would check the equipment and weather with his father before going on the water, but Abe was in the outpatients' clinic of the Carbonear hospital having elaborate tests done on his heart and kidneys. Hurrying to get ready, John misplaced his sweater and decided he would wear the coat. "That's a hard-looking piece of gear, old boy," Robert said, "but I do believe there's a touch of green in it." He had started spouting poetry as soon as he got in the car. To his embarrassment, John could find only one jigger and line in the boat; usually there were half a dozen. The others, he concluded, must be locked up in Abe's basement or on loan to a bona fide fisherman. During the past year, the trawl fishery had picked up a little. With just one jigger, there was some question whether they should go on the water at all, but Robert said it was being upon the enchafèd flood that interested him, not pursuing the creatures that swam in it. "Westward, ho!" he shouted after lunch, and they were soon off, heading due south to the Northern Bay shoals that John knew best.

By five o'clock they had jigged enough fish on The Grunt and Nelly's Ledge to make a respectable catch, and John decided to call it a day. The wind had freshened; the water was getting just a bit choppy. As Liam was pulling in the last fish, he slipped and lost the line over the side. John consoled him: Abe had lots more at home, he told the boy, it was only a fishing line, no big deal. "Keep her nose into the wind, Bob, while I start the Johnson," he said as he went aft. The poet had been addressing verses from the bow to the cliffs of Northern Bay for two hours. Now he took a paddle and turned his attention to the salt water slapping at the boat. He had sailed the seas and come, he said, to the holy city of Byzantium.

In the humdrum stern, the engine wouldn't start. John hauled on the lanyard with greater and greater force, checked the mixture, fiddled with the hose, and squeezed so much gas into the engine that a bluish halo spread around the boat. The engine was flooded, he said; not to worry. Liam and Declan sat side by side on the aft thwart, looking at their father. For his part, Robert gamely kept the bow into what he termed the blessed waves. The wind was rising as the day ended. John felt a few drops of rain on his face. He tried the lanyard a dozen more times. Not a sputter.

More drastic procedures were in order. He got the bucket of tools from the bow, took the plastic protective hood off the motor, and contemplated the flywheel, sparkplugs, and other appendages. There wasn't a lot that could go wrong with a Johnson. He removed the two sparkplugs with a socket wrench, cleaned the points of each with an emery board that Abe kept in a small watertight bag, screwed the plugs back in, reconnected the wires, and pulled again with considerable force on the lanyard. Two things happened. There was a slightly different, perhaps more hopeful, sound from the engine, the faintest inner bubble of noise that at least hinted at combustion; and the lanyard was torn loose from its groove on the flywheel, throwing John backwards over the gas tank and sculling oar, toppling the boys from their perch onto the codfish, and sending the lanyard itself flying off into the gong-tormented seas. Robert was still reciting. When John got up to look for the lanyard, it was nowhere to be seen.

The sun dropped behind the hills and threw an eerie brown light over the bay. All hands now searched for a small rope to improvise a lanyard. There was no such rope to be found in the boat. Abe had forgotten something! John cut off a piece of the four-ply nylon mooring attached to the emergency grapelin and tried to use one of the strands, but because of its rope-like configuration it wouldn't fit into the lanyard groove. He checked his own and his guests' clothes for belts, laces, or string, but found nothing he could use.

The boat was now drifting quickly offshore. He considered throwing the grapelin over the side, but decided against it for the moment. Panic rose in his throat, choking him. Nobody was looking for them on land. They were in nobody's pocket this time.

He went forward to check the fore cuddy again for even a discarded piece of string, but there was none. Then he moved aft once more, thinking he might spin the wheel without a lanyard, though he had never seen that done or heard of it being done. As he edged past the frightened children, he slipped again and fell against the gunwale. He felt something against his leg, something in the coat. Taking a knife, he slit the lining and found a neat roll of fishing line about a fathom long. How rotten was it? he wondered. He knotted the end, put it in the groove, and pulled. The line broke a foot from the knot. He tried a new knot and a gentler pull; again the line broke. He tossed it aside and dug deeper into the recesses of the coat, turning up a clownish hat and a piece of white cloth. The other contents were balls of wool and a handful of dirt.

He looked at Cape St. Francis at the mouth of the bay, towards which they were drifting. It was more than ten miles away; the little boat would never make it across in heavy seas. Then he thought he saw something reddish in the water. Was it possible? Out as far as this? Couldn't be. But he fancied he saw it again. He told everybody to watch for a float, but it was he who spotted it once more about two hundred yards downwind. He gave Robert a gaff and took one himself, then put out the sculling oar and tried to gauge where the wind was taking the boat. A wooden buoy went by before anybody had a chance to get it, though John lunged for it and skinned his arm badly. "Jesus, Jesus!" he yelled in a rage, then said, as calmly as he could, "That was the haul-up. See how fast it went by? Watch for the big float next. You won't see it until the last minute. Go for the rope under it if you can." Suddenly the plastic float was next to him, moving quickly. He dropped the oar, stabbed madly with the gaff, and caught the rope. It took all his strength to hold on as the boat's aft swung into the wind, driving water in over the engine. He hauled the float and a fathom of rope into the boat, moving forward as he did so and bringing the bow back into the wind. More water came over the side. He sent Robert aft to comfort his children.

It was a cod trawl with the markings of a fisherman named Jack Mulley from Burnt Point, a few miles below

Northern Bay. John had a reason for remembering the man. As a youngster, Jack used to ride the white horse at the head of the Orangemen's parade, and everybody envied him. The Burnt Point fishermen were beginning to move off their own grounds onto less crowded ones. Men were grumbling about this on the wharf in Ochre Pit Cove, but Abe thought the Burnt Pointers were fine workers. "Live and let live," he said.

The rope under the float was much too big for his purposes. Looking over the side, John saw two ropes stretching off into the depths. One, he knew, the mooring he had in his hands, went straight down to the heavy rock that held the outside end of the trawl in place on the shoal. The other, a smaller rope attached to the mooring a fathom below, went off at an angle to the trawl itself, an arrangement of baited hooks on a hundred and fifty fathom line, so contrived that it stayed just off the bottom and swung back and forth over the shoal with the changing tides. The whole contraption would be dragged by the boat in this wind, but it held her a little. He would have to work fast. Otherwise the boat might pull the trawl right off the shoal into deep water.

John hauled the mooring up until he got to the rope leading to the trawl. Though smaller than the mooring, that rope was also too big to make a lanyard. He would have to go deeper. He threw the float back in the water, leaned over the stem, and pulled towards the trawl itself, about twenty or thirty fathoms down in the swirling, black water. The haul-up rope, attached halfway down and used by the fishermen to get access to the trawl without having to disturb the mooring, came into his hands. It was again too big. He threw that aside and hauled away, coming at last to the knot between the rope and the trawl line. Glancing towards the shore, he could barely make out Ochre Pit Cove through the driving rain. His arms and chest ached. He could see a few hooks ahead of him. One had a small fish on it.

Partially anchored by the trawl, the boat was taking on more water. There was only one thing to do: he had to cut the trawl line. He tied the rope in the risings of the boat, then hauled two fathoms of the trawl aboard and hitched it over the stem. The fish turned out to be a sculpin. He cut off a fathom, and retied the line at the original knot. Jack would probably still find out that somebody cut his trawl. Fishermen knew these things.

"If I get her going," he said to Robert, "untie the rope and let it go. That's all you have to do. Don't let it go until the engine is working. It might take me three or four hauls."

"Why not just cut it?" Robert asked. "Give me the knife or the hatchet."

"No. It'd mess up his trawl, he might even lose it. Those things are hard to set. There's an art to them." John moved aft past his friend, then turned. "And if you mention the blood-dimmed tide or wine-dark sea, I'll strangle you when we get ashore."

He put a knot in the piece of line and laid it in the groove. At the first savage yank the engine caught and Robert, bouncing high in what was now a tumultuous and menacing ocean, released the trawl. "Off, helmsman, off!" he yelled, "Ireland is free. Put out to sea, put out to sea!" John waited a few seconds for the line to sink before putting the engine into forward gear.

On the way in, he looked at the fish they'd caught and saw it had been badly mangled by all the walking back and forth. He couldn't leave it in the boat overnight. It would have to be filetted as soon as they got in if any was to be saved. He'd need help because his sore arm was giving him a lot of trouble. It had to be held a certain way to keep the pain in check.

He felt like throwing the old coat overboard but decided that would be a foolish thing to do on such a cold evening. Besides, some use might still be found for it on shore. Even with the coat wrapped around him, his body shivered and stiffened as the boat headed for the wharf. The salt spray beating in over the bow stung his face and wet him through to the skin.

Dawnlight

Taking a shortcut to get to the meeting on time, Gus Fanning drove past the old Capitol Theatre in the downtown, where *A Touch of Class* was playing. His friend Robert Mullaly fell silent. "Glenda Jackson looks a little like Siobhan," Gus said. Robert hadn't mentioned his beautiful Irish wife since his arrival from Toronto a week before. That could only spell trouble. He now said gravely, "I too have been touched by something," and before a response could be given, turned to stare at the massive granite outcrop that loomed over the city to the south. "The hills, the black hills!" he exclaimed, as if seeing them for the first time. "There's nothing in Ireland like them, old boy. What a landscape for poetry!" In his enthusiasm, he rolled down the window, stuck his head and torso out, and waved his arms. The exact purpose served by this manoeuvre was not clear. A priest walking along Duckworth Street, thinking he had been recognized, waved back. Horns honked in a couple of passing cars. A dog barked.

"Touched by what?" asked Gus.

It being a cold afternoon in mid-March, the window was soon rolled up. There was a pause. Robert reached over and clutched his friend's arm. "'I stayed even in the woods and mountains'," he said, quoting somebody Gus didn't recognize, "'roused to prayer in snow, in frost, in rain'." Gus was already used to the long silences, interrupted by citations, curses, prayers, gesticulations, and shouts about Ireland that betokened a disordered spirit. Disordered but not broken, for Robert was turning up at pubs and parties, holding forth, rolling home in the wee hours. People were coming up to Gus in the supermarket and saying, in low tones, "You have a friend named Mullaly?" When he conceded that he did, indeed, have a friend of that name, the inquirer might say, "Colourful, isn't he?" "He is that," Gus would reply. With his cape and white goatee, not to mention his gift of the gab, Robert cut a dashing figure in dull old St. John's.

"What did you say, old man?" he asked. "Sorry, I missed that. My head was somewhere else."

"You said you had been touched. Touched by what?"

Robert smiled, hinting at deep conspiracy. "I'm not sure you'd understand, I haven't talked to you in so long. Seriously, I mean. How many years, twenty? It's not just a question of trust."

It had been eight or nine years, not twenty. But perhaps the point wasn't worth dwelling on. "Once in cahoots, always in cahoots," said Gus. This had been one of their phrases since the earliest days of the friendship, just after they ventured into university from the outharbours. It had stayed with them through their postgraduate years in London; and even afterwards when they went their separate ways, the cunning one to Ireland and Toronto, the other back to home ground in Newfoundland, it had found its way into letters and telegrams.

"By a hand, I guess," Robert said. "Hands. Yes, that will do. By enemy hands."

He didn't seem inclined to say more. Gus backed off, and silence reigned for five minutes as they fought the traffic. At last they were free. The road passed the railway station on Water Street west and swerved south, as if leaving the city and ocean for some secret inland valley of content. But it was only taking a quick route past the western suburbs along the side of a great rocky ridge, an extension of the Southside Hills that Robert so admired.

"You and I could only go so far," he said. "Do you know that yet? I know it. There was a lead on us from the outset, a halter. It brought me to where I am. You too, I suspect."

"We haven't done so badly," said Gus.

At Littledale, the former convent used by the church as a retreat house and conference center, they turned in and found a parking space. The panel discussion to which they had been invited was part of a three-day meeting on "The Possibility of a Newfoundland Literature," sponsored by a local writers' group. The theme of the panel was "Starting Up." Robert had been invited to attend by a drunken poet when it was discovered that he was an authority on the Irish literary renaissance. Gus cadged an invitation without too much trouble. Though primarily a teacher, he did a little writing.

At the registration desk, Robert declined to fill out the required form, causing a minor crisis that could be resolved only by the conference conveners. Someone went to find them.

"It's one of the ways they ensnare us," he confided to Gus. "Think how many forms you've filled out, old boy; how often you've been tested for credentials, handwriting, patience, grammar, eloquence, even addition and subtraction; how often you've had to consent to be judged by the powers above; how much time you've wasted filling in their stupid blanks; how often you've been found wanting. That's one of the ways you've been kept in your place. One of many."

At this point one of the conveners arrived and interjected a word of protest, but Robert ignored her. "Those who fill out forms and those who don't—that's the real division between people in the world, old man. It's a mental thing. Don't fill them out. Don't play the game."

He also refused to pay the registration fee, noting to Gus that "paying your way in" was a confession of lowliness, subjection. "That was how the British held onto their colonies for so long, by making the blacks and Irish and yellows pay to live in their own lands. The Brits finally got them to *want* to pay. That's colonialism, when you want to pay the thief who robs you, want to genuflect to his idols, want to teach his books to your own children, want to speak in his accent." Another official of the conference was summoned, there was a further relaxation of the rules. They got in free.

The "Start Up" session was now under way, and as they entered the main conference hall a young woman was haranguing the audience of about fifty on the lack of a "feminist thrust" in the literature of Canada. She was tall, blonde, bespectacled, dressed in black pants, grim, passionate. Robert strode to the front of the room and took a seat. Gus trailed behind, nodding apologetically to a few acquaintances on the aisles as he tiptoed past. "What little literature there is in Canada," she said, "and I daresay it's the same in the Maritimes and Newfoundland, though I can't say this for sure since I'm from B.C., is of the 'boy's own' variety, dealing with hunters, trappers, explorers, and the like.

Mostly men playing with their guns. The woman's touch is in some of it, but the woman's fist is missing." She enlarged on this point, calling for the appearance of a radical pro-woman literature "that wasn't afraid to deal with such erstwhile forbidden subjects as tampons and dish rags." She sat down to heavy applause.

Towards the end of the next presentation, which concerned the practical difficulties standing in the way of a writer starting up as a professional—buying the right word-processor, making contacts, dealing with editors and publishers, getting the proper training—Robert dozed off and began to slide off his chair. This, together with his heavy breathing, proved disconcerting to the speaker, an earnest young man with thick glasses whose mastery of the computer had made it possible for him to make a living by writing in distant Labrador, and while attempting to finish quickly he knocked some of his equipment off the table. The crash woke Robert up.

"Did that woman say 'tampons', old boy?" he whispered.

"She did," said Gus.

"And 'erstwhile', did she say that too?"

"Afraid so."

A mournful look came over Robert's face. "There's something happening here," he whispered. "Something minor, maybe, a room on the outskirts, a few people. But you can never tell."

He folded his arms, shifted around in his chair, and grunted so loudly that the chairperson asked if he wished to make an intervention. Gus knew her: Margaret Penman, author of sensual love poetry and successful local cookbooks. "I might have something to say later on, Madam," Robert said.

The third presenter, a British-born professor at the university, spoke of the importance of style and content. To her mind, how to put "the right words in the right places" could be learned only through study of the greatest writers in the language, Jane Austen, George Eliot, and Charlotte Brontë, for example. While local colour should be admitted, she hoped an alertness to ideas in the great world beyond the flakes would not utterly disqualify one from being considered a Newfoundland writer. Not that flakes didn't have a place; and stages too, and slipways, and even maggoty fish, she said smilingly. But the "big ideas" couldn't really be overlooked. One of those ideas was feminism, and she concluded by wholeheartedly supporting the first woman's presentation on that subject. "It's not just that women have been 'held back' in Newfoundland," she said, "they've been 'on their back' far too long." The audience was with her, and some shouted other jokes about backs as she returned to her chair. The session was growing animated.

The final speaker, whose homely looks belied her Marxist views, wanted to emphasize the political role of literature. She hoped that socialist ideas would appeal to the new writers, many of whom were in the audience. While "the masses need art of all kinds," the government should increase its support to small publishers and to writers, especially women writers, she said. She took second place to nobody present in her commitment to the rights of women. "I have suffered in the struggle," she said.

"She looks well fed to me," Robert muttered. Now that the formal speeches were at an end, he was sitting up, starting to get his second wind.

The chairperson called for comments from the floor. A question about the relative merits of hard and floppy disks used up three or four minutes. Gus noticed Robert was squirming, humming a little. The advantages of belonging to the Writers' Union of Canada were also outlined by someone, not without protest, however, from a gentlemen with a manuscript under his arm who thought the organization elitist. A point was raised about the importance of pressing editors to have fifty percent of the contents of St. John's magazines written by women. "Any other observations?" asked Ms. Penman. Robert turned and looked around the room. He waited about ten seconds. Then he rose to his feet.

His opening was courtly, generous. He complimented the organizers of the conference on their vision and daring, said many smooth things. Then he reminded the panel of the purpose of the conference—it was to discuss the idea of a Newfoundland literature, an important theme. He was himself, he said, a student of those who had started up the greatest literary movement of the twentieth century, Yeats, Joyce, Synge, and Beckett. These had gained inspiration and sustenance, "not, like Jonah, from the belly of the great devouring whale, not, I mean, from England's literature and history, but from their own sources, their own hills and valleys, their own people, their own rag-and-bone shop." He begged the gathering not to think that a literature could be built on imported goods. "Boycott, my friends, socialism, and Marxism, and feminism, and colonialism, and all the other—isms: 'those big words that make us so unhappy', as Joyce said. The so-called 'big ideas' we've heard so much of today were mostly spawned in the minds of drifters and malcontents in the boneheap of Europe, fifty, a hundred, two hundred years ago. What relevance have they to us, here, now? This is a new land. Why heed the slum-dwellers of London and Paris?"

"I conclude, Madam Chair, let me conclude." He had gone on far too long already, and there had been rumblings of opposition, hisses. His patience had been tested. Twice his voice had risen to put down growls of protest. Now it rose again. "I say, we must look to ourselves, write out of our own blood and guts and heart, not out of any regard for the tatterdemalion—isms that some vagabond adventurer rejected by his or her own country would have us bow the knee to. Joyce in fact said that 'until he has freed himself from the mean influences around him—every sodden enthusiasm—no man is an artist at all'. That was undoubtedly an extreme view. But if we must have sodden enthusiasms, let them be of our own sod." He sat down.

Not many clapped. Ms. Penman, stretching her role as chairperson a bit far, commented on what was to her mind the most singular feature of the remarks she had just heard: "He didn't mention the word 'she' once, and not one of the authorities and writers he cited, from Jonah to Joyce, was female. No doubt the whale was masculine too. You don't like —isms, Mr. Mullaly, but I'd call that good old male chauvinism."

Wild cheering followed. "That does it, old boy," Robert whispered to Gus as, red-faced, arms flying, he leapt to his feet again, demanding attention. "Madam Chair, I insist, Madam Chair...."

There was an uproar. "Sit down!" some in the audience screamed. "Oh, no!" "Get out!" "Chauvinist!" yelled others. "He thinks he's St. Patrick," someone cried.

"...it is time for me to take out my sword!" Robert shouted above them all.

Later when he was discussing the episode with a few friends, Gus had to confess that for a second or two the fancy struck him that Robert actually had a sword or dagger of some sort under his cape and was getting ready to lay about him like a Knight of the Red Branch. Jack Duff, a scriptwriter and novelist visiting from Toronto, said he wasn't sure what Robert was going to take out, but he thought it best to look through the window anyway, just in case.

"I say, it is time for me to draw my sword," Robert repeated, and the chairperson, seeing he would not yield, was forced to give him the floor again, to derisive groans from all present, except one. Robert allowed the hubbub to subside. He walked over to the panelists' table and stared at each of them. Then he turned and faced his tormentors. His arms were folded under his cape.

"I heard, as from a great distance, the name of Patrick flung at me—and not without reason, not without symbolic meaning, the day being what it is. I seize upon the name joyfully and thankfully, noting, Madam Chair, before expanding a little"—another groan was heard at this point—"that it is again a he I talk about. But for your sake may I mention Bridget too? And Deirdre of the Sorrows, and Queen Maeve, and Lady Gregory, Pegeen Mike, Eva Gore-Booth, Con Markievicz, Siobhan McKenna, Kate O'Brien, Claire Boylan...."

"Enough!" An anguished call.

"Ireland is an —ism too!" Another voice.

Robert had paused. He seemed to be twisting his hands under his cape. He looked at the ceiling. Gus was about to move to help him.

"All right. It is to Patrick, anyway, that I return...."

Still another yell. "We've had enough of him already."

"I must say my piece," said Robert. "I have been challenged. I will speak."

"Let him talk!" said Gus over the din, surprised at his own temerity. Silence of a sort ensued, though Gus thought it wouldn't last long.

Robert started again, slowly. "I give you Patrick, who at the age of sixteen came to Ireland a slave, and for six years tended the sheep of his captor in the mountains. He writes of it in his *Confession*. We can imagine the boy, far from home, across an ocean in the cold hills of Ireland, praying, waiting for the dawnlight, as he says."

He had caught them now. The silence was complete.

"One night as he slept he heard a voice saying, 'Rise up, and go!'"

At this point his wedding ring dropped to the marble floor, its small tintinnabulation drawing all eyes. It rolled slowly to the chairperson's feet. She picked it up and put it on the table near him. He made no move towards it. Was there a tear in his eye? A tremor in his voice? Could he go on?

"It is true, my friends, what is written: the movements that work revolutions in the world are born out of the dreams and visions in a peasant's heart on the hillside."

The last pause was a brief one. "'I was like a stone that lies in the deep mire', Patrick wrote, 'and he that is mighty came and in his mercy lifted me up'. There have been no hands lifting us up to freedom in Newfoundland; none lifting me up, that's for sure; the opposite. But by the grace of God we have our own hands, and if we don't use them to lift ourselves up, then we'll deserve, and richly deserve, the miserable little footnote in the back of the history books that might be our fate. Oh, let it not be our fate! Let us get out of the deep mire of mediocrity! To do so, we need only these, the hands of a Newfoundlander!"

He flung his cape open and raised his ringless hands heavenward, as Patrick might have done in Munster after explaining the mystery of the Trinity to barbarous Irish chieftains. Then he sat down heavily. Gus touched him on the shoulder to console him.

Now the applause was general. Hands went up for questions. "Good stuff!" "Well put!" people were saying. "More, more!" someone called from the back. But the chairperson stood up and said she had to bring the discussion to a close because it was time for the next panel, on "Deconstruction in the Canadian Context," to get rolling. If more comment on Dr. Mullaly's remarks was needed, it would, she felt, be welcome at tomorrow's plenary session. This quieted the audience. They started to drift out to the coffee room, many pausing to bestow praise on Robert as they departed.

The two old friends slipped away to the car. "That was a close thing in there," Robert said as they drove back towards the dark city. "I'll be surprised if anything comes out of it. Momentary enthusiasm on their part. Not up to it. Can't tell, though. Can't." He was mumbling. For a half mile he fell silent. Then he brightened. "It was a damn close thing. For a few seconds I didn't think I could pull it off. And I don't mean the ring." Looking down, Gus saw that the ring was back where it belonged. Robert looked at him and smiled. "You have to be foxy as well as passionate, old boy," he said.

The hawker

It had not been easy getting over to the North Shore from the other side of the bay, but he had heard so much about it from his poor father that he felt he had to come. His plan was to start in Western Bay, where he spent the first day scouting the territory and selling, and then head north on foot all the way to Grates Cove. He would try to get a boat back to Portugal Cove from there. Covering the dozen or so outports would take him about four days, supposing his supplies didn't run out before then. If they did, he would have to contrive some way to get home. The thought of being stuck with nothing to do in a place like this was more than he could bear.

So this was the shore where he was born and where he'd spent a good part of his childhood. He had time to have a good look around Western Bay. As he expected, the people were well disposed towards him because of his father. "Your Pa was good to me," one woman said. Pa: what a strange thing to call his stiff, English father. It was a nice enough outport, all things considered. Full of misery, of course, but then so was most of Newfoundland. Western Bay was, at any rate, an improvement on Ochre Pit Cove, where he began his second day's work, which in turn was better off than the comically named Smooth Cove and the South Side of Northern Bay. Conditions seemed to get worse the farther north he walked. And what a road! It was little more than a cow track, but having been duly warned, he'd put on his hobnail boots. Hobnail boots and a pressed suit were quite a combination for July travel. Summer hardly came to a coast like this. If he remembered right, this was one of the oldest Methodist circuits on the island. His father once told him that some old people over here would still talk of the eighteenth-century missionaries Coughlan and Thoresby. The dead didn't stay buried on this shore. That was tradition for you.

Though he naturally hadn't pushed it within his own charge, his ULH was selling well wherever he went in Conception Bay. He supposed that was because there was so much TB around. Not wishing to confine himself to TB houses, he also advertised it as a general tonic and pick-me-up, and many who were in good health bought some just to have in their homes. So good was he at salesmanship that he was thinking he might spend the rest of his life at it. He sold five bottles in Western Bay, including one at the manse where he was born. "Seeing who you are," the minister's wife said as she passed him the money. But he managed to sell only one in Ochre Pit Cove and two in

Smooth Cove. Fifty-two to go. Admittedly one sale in an entire community was pretty rotten, but money was money. He would need every cent for what he had in mind. The fare alone would set him back a lot.

There were no Irish in Ochre Pit Cove and not many, for that matter, in Western Bay. That partly explained the low take. The Irish, bless their hearts, went for his product more than other races. Why he couldn't say, since TB seemed to be evenly distributed in the population. It was just something he noticed. As well, when he came through Ochre Pit Cove, most of the men were out fishing, and the women didn't want to buy anything without their say-so. If he got the chance, he might come back some Sunday and do another canvass.

He took a break near some steep cliffs called The Highlands and ate a lunch of bread and cheese, given to him in Western Bay. A passing glimpse of the reefs at the foot of the cliffs made him gloomy. How could there be anything but grief on this grim edge of the continent? The savage pounding of wave after wave against cold, bleak rocks always sent chills through him. His mother said he was too sensitive. He was, too. Recently he had wept when reading about the sufferings of Brébeuf and the other Jesuit martyrs. Just thinking of some of the things they went through gave him the shivers.

After he got past the South Side of Northern Bay, he felt a bit better. There weren't many families on the South Side: some Woodrows, Butlers, and one by the name of Jacobs. All bought the ULH. He could hear a low, sobbing cough, more like a moan, upstairs in the Jacobs house. How weak were men's lungs! When he came to what was called the West End of Northern Bay—he again noted with amusement the homely and sometimes fancy names given to the little coves—he had good luck too with the Hogans, Mullalys, and all but one of the Howells. Edmund Howell, a fisherman with a skinny wife and two quite beautiful daughters, opened a bottle, sniffed the contents, and asked him point blank:

"What'd you put in that stuff, old cock? It smells like harse's piss."

This was unexpected. "The ingredients cannot be given out, my good man," he replied. "Many of our competitors would dearly love to know what is in our 'stuff', as you term it, but that is a trade secret. I must not divulge it. And believe me, there is nothing equine in it."

He said all this while chuckling inside, because the ULH was only the tips of spruce buds reduced through boiling to a vile concentrate and mixed with sarsaparilla and rum. The rum was to prevent freezing in the winter. It might have given the mixture a bit of a kick, too. These poor creatures needed a lift. Altogether it cost him about three cents a bottle to manufacture. Then there was the time spent brewing and selling it, which to be fair had to be taken into account in calculating profits. He had to be paid for his labour.

"I think you could well do with some as a tonic," he said to the reluctant Edmund, who was turning out to be a challenge. "And your wife looks peaked to me."

"Who, Bess?" the fellow shot back. "My son, she's deaf as a hatchet, and there's divil the thing can be done for her. I even had her up to Broad Cove to the doctor once. Wonderful man, could put an ass in a cat. Nothing he could do for her. Told me he couldn't; honest man, gave me the straight goods. Not like you with the harse piss. But don't you worry about my missus. She's tough. Like the staragons."

Didn't these people have a fetching way of saying things, though? He'd have a few stories to tell later. Some of them weren't bad to look at either, he thought, as he glanced at one of the Howells' black-haired daughters sitting sideways on the kitchen table. There were times he wished he knew more about outharbourmen, but when they were on rural circuits his parents had kept him and the rest of the family apart from other children to prevent their picking up accents. Even so, his St. John's acquaintances told him he had a trace of the bay in his speech.

He left the Howell household, alas, no richer than when he entered it, but secretly pleased that he had dealt firmly with the first resistance to the ULH he had met with among the North Shore pork-eaters, as they were called by some who thought them a hard bunch. They were as gentle as lambs. He walked quickly past the next few houses because they were close to shops and he knew the merchants wouldn't buy anything from him at full price. If the market was really promising around here, and he would know whether it was or not after a few more miles, he might have a wholesaler send out a consignment before the fall.

In the vicinity of the forge, he ran into more misery and sold bottle after bottle. The Sleeveen Road alone took four off his hands. Moores's Mash at the lower end of Northern Bay was equally productive, but he got nowhere with a family of McCarthys who owned the cooperage. He could now see the Catholic church in the distance and soon found himself in Long Beach. "You'll do wonderful down in Long Beach," a man named Neash Hogan up at the forge had told him. "There's not a good lung in the place." It was getting late, and he thought he would soon lock up his satchel and look for a place to spend the night. He'd pick out a clean house for that, of course. There was no sense taking more chances than you had to.

But when he hit the first house in Long Beach, he decided he might as well canvass all of it and start at Gull Island in the morning. At this rate, he mightn't have to go beyond Job's Cove. Neash Hogan had been right. Long Beach was a bonanza. He had never encountered such dreadful sickness. Down a road called the Cash Lane he saw what he could only call walking skeletons in some houses. Death had stalked through this outport and cut a wide swathe. Not only the old, not only women and children, but men in the prime of life had felt the stab in the gut. As far as he could tell, very little had been done to fight the disease. Well, at least they could have the ULH. That was better than nothing. It was a drop of hope. That's what he had in his bottles. When he considered what he was doing, he always cheered himself with that thought. And who said hope couldn't cure?

He always blew his nose hard and hawked after he came out of a TB house, though if he ever picked up the germ he guessed there was little hope of clearing his chest of it in those ways. He hoped to God he wouldn't pick it up. Surely He would look after His own. Every now and then he checked his spit to see if there was any red in it.

He reached the bottom of Cash Lane and paused for a minute to look at the kelp on the beach, which was the colour of blood. A few fishermen were still working at this late hour. Rather than walk along the edge of the cliff, something he had never enjoyed doing, he went back up the lane and took the rough road by the graveyard. He noted the signs of fresh digging. Yet the graveyard was full of wild roses. He had read somewhere that the early explorers in Newfoundland had been astonished by the abundance of wild roses they saw at the edge of the cliffs. Yet perhaps they were everywhere in Canada, too. He would make a point of looking.

There were only two houses opposite the graveyard, and he made a sale at each. He then came to a lane leading to a big yellow house about two hundred yards from the salt water. This would be his last business call for the day, although it wasn't the end of Long Beach. But he was tired. He sat on a rock halfway down the lane to catch his breath. It was a warm, still summer's evening now, with hardly a trace of wind and only a murmur sounding from the groundswell and the distant, rolling waves. Cape St. Francis and Bell Island across the bay picked up the last of the sun's rays. The rondo of dusk, he thought. There were times when he was quite overcome by nature. Occasionally, he even liked the look of clumps of ice and seagulls. He would miss all this later, maybe.

At the bottom of the lane he walked through a clumsy wooden gate to the front of the house, picking his way through pigs, goats, and hens that rushed up to him, no doubt in the hope of getting a scrap of food. With some distaste, he noticed animal manure all over the front yard. He took care to get none of it on his boots. An almost toothless young woman, out of breath and flustered, answered his firm knock. "Come in, sir," she said even before he introduced himself. He entered the kitchen through a large porch that was filled with the odour of freshly-baked bread. He saw the brown loaves on an oilcloth-covered table on the way in, and his mouth watered.

Yes, the woman said, she had a son upstairs with lung trouble. That took care of one thing; he couldn't stay here for the night, bread or no bread. He soon pocketed the usual price and, though he declined tea, was sitting by the Waterloo stove in the rocking chair eating a slice of hot buttered raisin bread—he thought he could risk that—when the door opened.

A stocky fisherman came in. He wasn't tall, but anybody could see he had the strength of a six-footer. He had a jaw like a granite cliff, bright foxy hair, and flashing blue eyes. A smell came from him of tar, sweat, and oakum. A good smell.

"Who the Christ is this, Min?" the man asked, as he sat down heavily next to his wife on the wooden settle. "I'm just in off the water. Where's John Joe? Katie?" He took a boot jack from under the settle and started hauling off a rubber boot. "I told you before, I don't want them going to other houses. They should be home by this time. It'll soon be dark."

"My name is Mr. Edwin Pratt, my man," said the visitor cheerfully before the woman had a chance to answer, "and I'm here selling the Universal Lung Healer, created especially for the benefit of the sick and sickly in Newfoundland." This was the opening to his usual pitch. The sale had been made, but for once words failed him and he couldn't think of anything else to say. Then he added: "In fact, I've already sold a bottle to your good missus." He smiled as he said this and made a slight bow towards the woman. He was enjoying the bread and the warm kitchen. He almost wished he had taken the molasses she had offered. It was common; still, he had tried it once and liked it.

"The youngsters are gone into Long Beach Pond," the woman said. "They're trouting or something."

"So you bought a bottle, did you Min?"

"I did so, Will," she replied quickly. "'Tis for Billy Jim. Two dollars is a lot of money, but I got the life frightened out of me, honest to God, Will. Nothing is working on him, and he's special to me. I'm thinking he's going to die."

"And so he might, Min," the big fellow said gently, "and so he might, girl. Let's hope we only lose one. Pad lost six of his."

"Oh, is Ursie gone too?" she asked. "I didn't hear."

"Perished this morning, Lord have mercy on her." Then he looked away from her. "Turned six a week ago." He tackled the second boot.

"Some is going to St. John's, Will. A few Gull Islanders, I heard, one girl from Job's Cove. We could send Billy Jim over there."

"We could, yes, we could, certainly we could. And then what would the rest of us do for the winter? Go on relief? Go door to door?" She made no answer.

"Now, Mr. Edwin Pratt," the man said, "how old are you, might I ask?"

Why not tell him? "Twenty-five."

"Twenty-five? A young man. A fine, strapping young man. And what do you do for a living, Mr. Edwin Pratt, apart from selling syrup to consumptives?"

Was there an irony intended in this? Surely not. Yet he felt a shiver of fear. His sensitivity again. "I'm a probationer in the Methodist mission. On the Bell Island-Portugal Cove charge." He was almost finished the bread. Would he ask for more? With molasses this time? "I'm there on a temporary basis," he added.

"Oh, are you now? Temporary, are you? Well, well, well." The fisherman spoke slowly, as if he were in a dream. His rubbers were off, and there was a glassy look in his eye.

He looked at his wife again, and touched her hand. "Get a bit of supper for me, girl," he said. "I'll be in the stage till twelve o'clock tonight." He gestured with his head. She got up slowly and went into the porch, closing the door behind her.

Then, softly, after a pause, pointing: "Mr. Edwin Pratt, do you see that long tom over on the wall?" Of course he saw it. He nodded. It was a well cared for rifle by the looks of it; of great use, he imagined, in these parts when the "swiles" came ashore on the spring pack ice, as his father had told him was their wont. He had seen an antique one something like it in a house on Bell Island and one day asked the owner if he could buy it. He knew a merchant in St. John's who was building up a collection. But the school teacher in Portugal Cove had the same idea and had already laid claim to it.

"And this knife. Do you see that?" The man had picked up a knife, perhaps from under the settle. It was a cutthroat, used to cut the cod's throat and gills and slit its belly prior to gutting. It looked razor-sharp.

"Yes, I see it, certainly I see it."

"I'm not sure what I'm going to do with you," the man said. "I'm half tempted to shoot you between the eyes and heave your carcass over cliff for the dogs and maggots." He ran his thumb along the edge of the knife. "But before I do anything, you're going to do something for me. Put your hand in your pocket right now and give me back the two dollars you robbed from my woman. If you don't, I'm going to cut your ears off and use them for bait. That's as sure as my name is Will Flaherty." He said this in a soft voice.

The money was passed over. One of Jogues' priests had a skewer pushed up under his skin from his hand to his elbow. The trials of a man of God!

"Now get the hell's flames out of here," the man said, his voice rising at last. There was nothing wrong with *his* lungs. "No, not that way. That's not good enough for a gentleman like you."

He was escorted, not through the porch, but into the front hall off the parlour. The house's second, more substantial door, used only when the quality came calling or a body was taken out in a box, was unlocked and opened. He tried to maintain his dignity, but the fisherman actually lifted him by his scruff and pants, gave him a sharp kick, and sent him flying headlong into the dirty yard. He had forgotten his satchel! It came flying after him, bottles rattling inside.

"And if you so much as poke your nose into my house again, you'll get more than a lash in the arse," the fisherman said. "I'll damn well have you tarred and feathered." He slammed the door shut.

Oh, they were savages down this way! Worse than the bloody Iroquois!

Maiden aunt

After a wait of an hour or two, sometimes longer if it had been raining and the roads were muddy or if icy weather had made them slippery, they would see the lights of a car on the highlands three miles away and Jimmy or Colin would race down the lane to tell the family she was coming. It might take the taxi another half hour to get to lower Long Beach, because there were sometimes important passengers to be let off in Northern Bay. But then the car would turn the corner by the graveyard and she would arrive: suitcases and parcels were tumultuously unloaded; Max Morris, her slave, was paid his fare for the hundred-mile trip; and the taxi, full of the exotic smells of leather, rum, and cigarette smoke, would head down the shore, leaving Jimmy and his brothers and sisters in darkness at the top of the lane. Down this narrow track, not innocent of cow dung and similar perils, they now had to conduct their Aunt Agnes in her high-heeled shoes and fancy clothes. The children surrounded her, each carrying a piece of luggage or package, subdued in her presence. She had come only for the weekend, and they were excited that she had brought so much with her. Despite what experience had shown, they hoped most of it was for them.

"How's Ma?" Always her first question. Their grandmother lived in the Byrne house.

"Good."

"Your father?" He was her youngest brother.

"Number one."

"Your mother?"

"Ok, I guess," someone would say. Their mother sometimes got a bit cross when Aggie came to visit.

"Will John?" No answer. Though their uncle lived only a few hundred yards away, the two families hadn't been on speaking terms for years. It was a fraternal quarrel that went far back in the Byrne family history. Aggie knew this, but always asked about Will John anyway and made a point of going to see him on her visits. Jimmy hadn't been inside the other Byrne house since he was five, when his uncle had taught him to read from old copies of the London *Times*.

Aggie might then ask about one or two of her great friends from Gull Island.

Finally: "How are ye getting on in school?" They'd be at the gate by this point.

"Good."

The warm house then received them, where she distributed her gifts of candy, oranges, and sweet biscuits for the children, cigarettes and something stronger for the adults. It was on one of her visits, latterly when he was in grade ten, that Jimmy first saw gin. She drank it with hot water and sugar. It smelled like juniper berries. Even with sugar, he thought, it had to have a sour taste.

It was always better waiting for her than actually having her in the house. Not that she ever came without presents. But keeping watch for the headlights was the best part, no matter what she brought. Her gifts, moreover, were of a certain character; edible, never playful. Her relationship with the Byrne youngsters, Jimmy realized much later, was the formal one of duty. She didn't coddle them, and when she gave them things, she expected gratitude and quiet in return. Having children underfoot was not her vocation. At times she got their names mixed up.

It wasn't until he was older that Jimmy also came to see what cargo, beyond candy and liquor, she carried into their lives in the declining outport of Long Beach. But he had some sense of it even then. The sight of a middle-aged woman smoking, drinking, and holding her own in arguments with men—there seemed to be more of them around when she visited—made an impression on him. Her loud, husky, laughter reverberated through the house, whose old timbers were used to softer sounds. He noticed that her presence affected the status of their father. What he said wasn't the law, to her. She paid no heed to their taboos and grievances. As head nurse in the St. John's Sanatorium, she moved in a larger sphere, moved easily, on her own terms. To the children, her example was a shining one, extending the range of what was possible. Yet it was unsettling too, for it subtly loosened the ties that bound them to the familiar and available pleasures of their narrow world.

In Jimmy's first two years of high school, her visits were less frequent, and in his final year, she didn't come at all. He would hear his mother and father speak of her in low tones: she was travelling, with whom or for what purpose was not disclosed; she was sick, then better. Or was she better? Some doubt was expressed. Letters arrived from foreign places, letters not shared with the children. Jimmy knew she was pressing to have him and Colin go to St. Bon's College in St. John's to take grade twelve as boarding students. Neither one of them had been to the city before. Indeed, they had gone only once as far as Carbonear, twenty miles up the shore.

It was in their third week at St. Bon's that their aunt again entered Jimmy's and Colin's lives. They were now starting to get used to the harsh discipline of the Christian Brothers' school and the tough curriculum of the advanced grade. A boarder's life was grim, especially if weekend visits home weren't possible. Boys from Bell Island or Holyrood might escape; most wouldn't get away until Christmas. Before the third Spartan Sunday had to be endured, the head of the boarders, Brother Bowen, approached Jimmy one evening after rosary.

"Byrne, you got an aunt working in the San?"

"Yes, Bro."

"She run the joint?"

"Don't know, Bro."

"She wants you to go in for dinner Sunday, with that brother of yours. What youse people call dinner." Brother Bowen was an American in exile.

"Yes, Bro."

"That's against the rules. Boarders aren't allowed out for meals on weekends, unless it's to their own home. You know that?"

"Yes, Bro."

"If I change the rules for youse guys, I gotta change 'em for everyone. You know that?"

"Yes, Bro."

Brother Bowen looked at him sourly. Jimmy had got on the wrong side of him once already, by mispronouncing Chicago. "I hope you do, bud, I just hope you do. But I'll make an exception in this case. You and Colin have permission to go, every Sunday until the end of term. Unless you lose more than four points the week before. If you do, you can't go. I don't care if the prime minister phones up. Got that?"

"Yes, Bro." Every week the boarders were given cards with ten spaces, one or more of which was crossed and initialled by any Brother spotting a fault in their clothes or behaviour. Each point lost beyond four meant an hour taken away from the precious free time on Saturday and Sunday afternoons.

"Be back in time for the rosary, twenty to six. Y'hear, wise guy?"

"Yes, Bro."

"And there's no need to broadcast this to the other boarders. Ok, smart ass?"

"Yes, Bro."

The idea that the rules of St. Bon's were capable of being bent for any purpose had not occurred to Jimmy before.

And so a weekend custom was established that, in fact, lasted for the whole year. They would leave St. Bon's in time to get a Bowring Park bus at one o'clock, reaching the Sanatorium a half hour later or, if the bus was late, by two o'clock. Aggie would often be watching through the window of her apartment in the nurses' residence as they got out at Hamlyn's store, opposite the main entrance. She knew Mrs. Hamlyn personally; indeed, she seemed to know everybody in the west end of St. John's. At first, she would meet them in uniform, talk to them briefly, and then phone the hospital kitchen for plates of dinner. Big servings of turkey or beef with vegetables would be produced, together with glasses of milk and bowls of custard. Once there was lemon meringue pie, a special treat. Second helpings were available, a thing unheard of at St. Bon's. When they finished, another phone call brought someone to take the dishes away, and Jimmy and

Colin would sit around reading her books until four o'clock, when they left to be sure to make it back in time for the rosary. On snowy or rainy days, Mrs. Hamlyn let them wait inside the store for the bus.

While they read her books, Aggie would leave to go on her rounds in the hospital. Different books would be laid out on the card table each week. It was in her living room—the bedroom they took to be off limits—that Jimmy first tackled A.J. Cronin's novels, *Thirty Days to a Better Vocabulary,* the *Imitation of Christ* of Thomas à Kempis, and Merton's *Seven Storey Mountain.* The last two were hard going. Aggie had scribbled notes on many pages.

A sense of her mastery was conveyed in the way her orders were promptly obeyed. The kitchen staff and nurses jumped when she said jump, and it wasn't as if she forced them to do what she asked; they wanted to do things for her. Though there was someone called Matron to whom she deferred on rare occasions, it was clear that she had great authority. She was surrounded by drama. Nurses rushed to her with questions. Phone calls would come through to her bedroom, announcing some trouble on the wards. On their first visit the phone rang a few minutes after their arrival. They could hear her. "Yes.... No! Too bad, I thought she'd last a bit longer, but there you are. We'll have to send her home.... No, she's got to have something decent to be buried in. There's nothing for her down north, where she's going. Remember, it's an outport, my dear. I've got a dress that's not too bad. Come over and get it. Shoes, too. Can you get me some stockings and underwear? ...No, there's nobody with me. Two boys, that's all.... All right. Phone for the casket, the cheap one, we'll get the money somewhere.... No, I don't want to do it, you do it." A nurse soon came in and went to the bedroom, leaving with a brown bag under her arm.

When they left each week she gave them two dollars each, to add to the modest weekly allowance they received from their parents. Jimmy saved the money and bought the

St. Joseph's Daily Missal, greatly favoured over other missals by the Brothers. Colin generally lost his money playing poker. He was getting a reputation in the school. Once he borrowed the missal and, seeing that the mass for the day was that of "a virgin, not a martyr," went looking for one of a martyr, not a virgin. That was the one he wanted to read, he said. He spoke out a couple of times against the Latin mass in religion class. As the term wore on, he became less willing to go to the San, but the two dollars drew him. One weekend, Aggie treated a black eye he'd been given by a tough boarder from Placentia Bay, who'd lost a front tooth in the exchange. "I hope his gob is sore for a month," she said; then added, to Jimmy, "Colin's not so bad as he lets on."

On the first Sunday after the Christmas break, Jimmy went to see her alone because Colin had lost too many points. Aggie spent most of the afternoon on the wards and missed her calls. The telephone rang again and again. At last Jimmy, who was trying to read an article in the *Catholic Digest* on proofs for the existence of God—he was studying apologetics, and having a hard time with it—went into the bedroom, picked it up, and said "Hello." The bed was unmade. Books, letters, and prayer beads were spread over the sheets. Medicine bottles and other objects were on the bedside table by the phone.

A man's voice was on the line. "Ag, I can't make it tomorrow," he said. "The usual reason. Nothing special; you know I want to come, I just can't. Phone you next week when I get back from the north."

"I'm not Aggie," said Jimmy, miffed that someone had taken him for a woman.

There was a pause. "Who are you, then? What are you doing there?"

"I'm her nephew, Jim Byrne." He decided then and there to try to change his name to give it more of an adult ring. "I'm just in getting my dinner." Should he have said that? Was he allowed to be in here at all, eating hospital food? Was this an inspector he was talking to?

"Oh, sorry," said the man. "I'll call back." Then he hung up.

A half hour passed; still no Aggie. The phone rang again, and when Jimmy answered there was a click on the other end. On being told of the calls, Aggie said with a laugh, "It's nothing. Forget it. Now you tell Colin to watch his bobber and come in here next week to have a decent meal. I want you to know what good food is like." She had hurried back to see him before he left for the bus and was out of breath. He noticed she had lost some weight. She was a big woman, always dieting.

Three weeks passed before they made it back to see her. St. Bon's was playing the Feildians in senior hockey the first Sunday, a game they didn't want to miss. The Brothers urged all the boarders to come out and cheer for the team. It was more than just a hockey game, they said. Though behind 4-1 at the end of the second period, St. Bon's fought back and won 5-4. The following week they both lost too many points. Jimmy had been walking outside the boarders' common room, when Brother Caine met him and accused him of crawling through the window. He denied this, but the Brother scratched off the rest of his points anyway, confining him to quarters for the whole weekend.

After classes on Monday, Brother Bowen spotted him in the corridor just after he had written a rough test in social problems. He was doing his best to make sense of Malthusian theory and economic principles, but the subject was new to him.

"You didn't go to see your aunt yesterday, Byrne," the Brother said.

"No, Bro. I had to stay in. Brother Caine took off eight points for crawling through the common room window, and I didn't even do it."

"You sure you didn't?"

"Yes, Bro."

"Yes what?"

"Yes, I didn't do it."

"How many youse lost this week?"

"One. Somebody messed up my bed." Jerome McIsaac did it. Jimmy would find a way to get him back.

"Ok. Don't lose any more, y'hear, Jimbo? Your aunt called up Brother French." Brother French was the principal. He and Brother Bowen didn't get along.

"Yes, Bro."

"One more thing. If you lose more than four again, let me know. I might be able to do something. Not for Colin, just for you. Keep that to yourself, y'hear?"

"Yes, Bro. Colin's not so bad as he lets on, you know." But Brother Bowen shook his head and walked away.

The next weekend was free for both of them, but Colin won eight dollars playing Chicago on Saturday morning and didn't want to go in. "Tell her I lost ten points," he said. Jimmy did so, although he thought she'd find out. She was out of uniform this time and stayed with him, watching him eat. Her smoking made her cough. There were pill boxes and gauze bandages around the living room, and he had to put some of the gear on the table to get a place to sit down. When the phone rang she jumped up to answer it, and he listened: "Yes.... Oh, hello.... Just a second, before we get into that.... Now hold on, I've got something to say to you too. I have to close the door, hang on." She put the phone down and came out. "I'll be with you in a few minutes," she told Jimmy. With the door closed he couldn't hear anything, but he was reading a book called *The Green Hat* and didn't mind being alone. When she came out an hour later, her eyes were red and puffy. She had little to say to him before he left.

He missed the next week because he had special classes with Brother Murphy on calculus. Math was giving him and Colin a lot of trouble, but Colin wasn't one to worry and went off to see a girls' basketball game on Sunday afternoon, skipping the extra class. Jimmy had come fifth in his class at Christmas and knew that unless his math picked up he'd do no better in the finals. There was even a danger of dropping below fifth, if he didn't hold his grades in the subjects he was best at, English and French. The four ahead of him weren't slacking off, and Ears Kavanagh was starting to catch him.

Now came the retreat week for Lent. Brother Bowen caught him reading Llewellen's *How Green was my Valley* in study period.

"What's this?" he asked.

"A book, Bro." This slipped out.

"I can see that, wise guy. Is it part of your courses?"

"No, Bro."

Brother Bowen picked it up. "This a western?"

"No, Bro. It's about Wales."

"What about them?"

"Not the fish. The country."

"Oh. Where'd you get it?"

"My aunt loaned it to me."

"The one at the San?"

"Yes, Bro."

The Brother cleared his throat. "All right. Put it away. This period is for study, y'hear?"

"Yes, Bro."

Ten minutes later Brother Bowen was back. "You know something, big mouth? The whale is not a fish at all. It's an animal. You're not so smart."

"Yes, Bro."

"Yes, what?"

"I meant no, Bro."

"That's better. See me after. Colin too."

"Yes, Bro."

The discussion that followed was on the ten points that Colin said he'd lost two weeks before. Aggie had phoned Brother French about them. The cards were checked and the double lie easily discovered.

It was certainly a strapping offence. Brother Bowen merely grinned. "I'm not going to lay a hand on youse guys," he said. "Go and face your aunt on the weekend."

But when they went she was glad to see them. "Sure that's nothing, a few lies," she said, chuckling. "I've told hundreds myself, thousands. I'll let ye off this time. Hark now, don't do it again." They talked this over on the way back on the bus. Why hadn't they been punished? They couldn't figure it. "Bugger Bowen straps me if I don't piss straight," Colin said. Jimmy noted one other thing on their visit: the phone hadn't rung once.

Soon sports day rehearsals were taking up all their Sundays and, with that and the approach of the dreaded final exams, Jimmy didn't get to the San until two weeks before the end of term. She was in bed when he came in, and a nurse was looking after her. His meal was sent for once more. He did his best with it, but the food was no longer appetizing to him and he ate only half a plateful. She then came out of the bedroom in her nightgown, sent the nurse off on an errand, and sat looking out the window. She was drinking something from a cup. "Oh, bitter, bitter!" she said as she tasted it. Any kind of movement seemed to make her wince.

"Why don't you heat it up and put sugar in it?" asked Jimmy.

She smiled. "Oh, no, that's not the kind of stuff I got here. Wish it was." She took another sip, and grimaced. "I have to drink every drop in the damned cup." Then she sat back and looked at him with gentle eyes. "Don't be afraid, never be afraid," she said for no reason that he could see. "Now, my lad, you stay around for a bit and talk to me. I was here by myself the whole morning."

And he did stay, thinking it was his duty to do so. He talked until it was twilight. In the distance he could see the red sign light up on Hamlyn's store and the buses go by to the centre of town. It was well past seven o'clock when he rose and helped the nurse get her back to the bed. He said he would come again next Sunday, his last, and bring her something. His idea was to get her a flask of gin. Colin would know how to get his hands on one.

After he said goodnight, the nurse opened the door for him and started to explain how to get back to the school. He was a little scared at what he'd done, but then he thought, what the hell. "I know how to get there," he said. "Don't worry about me." He walked out towards the red light in the warm evening air.

Thing

It was high time for me to make something. I was forty-five and I'd been collecting for years. I had the materials in my attic; awls, horse comb, hoops, black wax, last, the lot. I even had a rasp that was used in the olden times to file down a horse's tooth if, say, one was out of line. Bet you haven't seen one of those. And I had a tool to give a horse a pill. Now that was a strange looking object. But if you were ever invited into my house, and I have to say that I don't have many visitors, you'd think that much of what lay around you was queer. None of it was new. No sir, I went in for only tried and untrue materials, the proven methods. Give me the old ways of undoing things, I always said. If I ever made a thing, people would recognize it, I thought. "Oh look, there's Gus's thing going up the road," I fancied they'd say as they stood in their driveways oiling their lawnmowers or swinging their whipper-snippers, "and what a fine one it is. What a dandy thing he put together."

Not that there wouldn't be a few flaws. There were bound to be some: a short tendon in the shank, perhaps, creating a limp, or the teeth wouldn't be just right despite the rasp, or the mane would be off. The mane had to ripple in the wind and shimmer in the sun. That's hard to do. Try it. The fetlock could be hard to nail down, as usual. For that matter, the whole design might be off a touch. Listen, pal, I'm no architect. The big picture gives me trouble. Always has. Turning corners, too, has never been easy for me. I'm a detail man by nature. And even some of those...well, enough said.

By forty-five, as you can imagine, I'd already done a lot of chiselling and hammering. A few fires had been lit from my shavings, I can tell you! I turned out what looked like a thing once, when I was about thirty-seven, but it was no good and I broke it up. You can tell right away when they're no good. Don't ask me how. You just know. So I took the hatchet to that one and started again. I started dozens of the buggers. Scores. Not that the start-up stage is easy. Nothing is. For me, anyway.

Then, at last, I made one. You can picture my feelings the day I opened the door and sent it on its way. And even before that, just looking at it in the workshop under my attic gave me a lot of pleasure. I made that, I said to myself. Believe me, for many years I despaired of doing it.

Could it whinny? Is that what you're thinking of asking me? Damn right, it could. That's just for starters. It can do a lot more than whinny, mister. Pay attention as it goes by and you'll see what I mean.

It got to the end of the lane and I called it back to make a few minor adjustments in the rump. There are always adjustments. Who do you think I am, God? I turned a few screws, no more. I mean, it was complete. Then I let it go again and watched as it stepped over the cow-catcher, shiny and, after a fashion, new. I'd never seen a walk like that, or a toss of the head. It made its way through the nearby meadows and I lost sight of it.

What did I do then, you ask? Tinkered some more, naturally. After all, I had the whole ark to get through, and now that I'd finished one, I had other ideas. Of course, I also waited for the good news to drift in from the fields of praise. See, I knew it was a true thing I'd made. Trust me, I'd really made one of the suckers.

Someone did phone me the day after I sent it out. Her name was Linda, actually. "I saw your thing," she said. "It went past me on Water Street yesterday, heading west. I'm glad you're building them. I think it's good for you."

She thought I was doing it for my health. I thanked her for calling, you know, made the usual noises, observed the niceties. Good for me! I whacked my forehead with the palm of my hand, getting blue paint on the grey hair above my ear. I was fashioning a robin's egg at the time. Another start-up. I slammed my fist on the workbench, rattling a cage with a lesser yellowlegs in it. Had a fancy about one of those, too. Good for me! Making that mother just about killed me. Blood, it cost me. Hey, listen, I'm not talking in metaphors here. I'm talking corpuscles, plasma. Come in one day, if you can squeeze in past the sets of hames and other tackling in the porch below my workshop, and I'll show you the scars. All over me. That son of a gun kicked like a mule. Oh, my foot! It trod on me there. My eye! It swished me with its tail one day when I was rough with the carding. And the loins: don't even ask. It's not funny, making things, though I have to say it can be engrossing. Good for me! I could kill Linda. I have ways of doing that. Might do it yet.

Then another friend reported. Percy I think it was, or Peter. One of them: I forget which. Anyway, he'd seen the thing too, in Mount Pearl, some miles from the capital. Had it gone so far to be seen by my sisters, I wondered? I have two in there, three some days. Probably not. It was still going west when he saw it—Percy or Peter, whoever—trotting past the yuppies in Newtown, one of the suburbs. Some chance of their having a peek at it!

"It's too small," he said. Nice enough in its way, good belly, gaskins, hooves, but a cut on the short side. That was how he put it. "How many hands is it?" he asked, again showing off his command of the terminology. I told him. "Hmmm," he said, clearly implying that anybody could make a thing as small as that. I know a clear implication when I hear one. In his view, evidently, it was just a matter of sitting down with the awl and wax, and getting the bits right. Bit.

Too small! "Have you seen the Tara Brooch?" I felt like asking him but didn't. Is that pin big? So the Mona Lisa is enormous, is it? Are the Bard's sonnet's long? Have a gander at Simon Bening's miniatures of March and June in the British Museum, dated c.1561. Are those large? Yet are not whole farmyards contained in them? Villages, even? Come on, let's talk business, I wanted to say, but didn't. How big is big? Let's get into this.

You're right, I'm touchy on that subject. Talk about sweeping vistas or weighty themes sets my teeth a-grinding. But I've seen full-rigged ships in rum bottles, sailing on stormy seas. That's the next job of work I'm half tempted to try. Not with ships; that's not my gig. You think it's easy to put a thing in there? Go ahead, get your pickaxe. I'll give you the bottle and materials. I have bottles in the storeroom under my porch.

A few who watched the thing go down their road phoned to say: you got something belonging to me in it. That reel of thread I loaned you last year, that's the left eye. Give it back. The pestle hanging down between the legs was in my mother's pantry six months ago. The purse you used for the scrotum is missing from my front room. The front right shoe you took from over my door.

One acquaintance named Withers, an impudent fellow, said that on its way through Kelligrews it came and peeped through his window. "Tell that thing to stay out of my life," he hissed into the phone. "Rein it in, man, corral it before you get in trouble." I had met the chap only twice. The first time was at the racetrack, where he gave me a hot tip—unasked for, I should say—on a nag that came in dead last, costing me twenty-five dollars. Afterwards, when I heard him complaining about verisimilitude at a showing of *The Black Stallion*, I seized him by the collar to remonstrate with him. Extreme, I admit, but the muzzle was off that night. And verisimilitude! Can you blame me?

And now he reappeared amidst the strong objectors.

"Oh, lectors and hearers!" I felt like shouting, but didn't. Be less vain. Your buttons and zippers will not be looked for by the great world. Your reel is unreal now, your discarded pouch a hardy set of equine ballocks. Besides, the thing is no longer mine, let alone yours. It strides west, apparently. Look at it, finding its own way. Out of dead parts, shades, borrowed things certainly, pieces of twine, old leather, scavenged objets d'art, was it stitched together, glued with sweat and tears, given life by—but I must hold back the secret ingredient, though one other knows what it is. Now it walks, does it not? Yes, walks. Rejoice with me.

But most of my neighbours and acquaintances didn't see the thing at all. "What!" I felt like exclaiming, but resisted the temptation. You didn't see it walk past your garage, Pozzo? Past your fish and chips shop, Kate? Across your lawn, Harry? It was close to you, Harry. But I knew Pozzo was gas-barbecuing in back, Kate sunning in back on her patio, Harry swimming or gazing in his new pool; and the thing has to come in through the front. My neighbours missed it, in short. If Harry had seen it in the distance, he'd have given it only a quick glance. I know that. And if he'd said anything, it would've been this: "It's only a damned old thing. There are thousands more like it." He wouldn't have said that to me, you understand, but to his own crowd.

Am I being too severe? Is the muzzle needed again? All right, he wouldn't have said thousands. He'd have said hundreds.

There aren't hundreds like that baby, Harry my boy.

The thing was across Cabot Strait when I last heard of it, maybe going to New Waterford, Nova Scotia, where I have relatives working in the mines. Or to my contacts in Fredericton, New Brunswick. I'm just guessing. It might well be on its way to Toronto, and I can hear the types up there now: "The old way of making them"; "I see a touch of craft in the stifle, and nowhere else"; "Back to the drawing board"; "I know a filly just like it"; "Major malfunction."

Poor thing! So few openings, so many grudges surfacing, so many stable boys waiting, whips in hand. It's better, I think sometimes when I'm gloomy, to keep your thing in the green stables—supposing that were possible—or even send a nose out to walk the streets instead, as someone did before me. But it has to be set loose finally to live. It just has to be. Don't ask me why. And a few of those locked gates might swing ajar. Someone could reach out, grab it, and haul it into his city. That still happens.

There are gifts inside that thing; little ones, granted. I know. I unmade them and put them there.